P9-DWZ-366

NINE MONTHS

Jasmine

by Maggie Wells

E

EPIC
Press

Jasmine
Nine Months: Book #3

Written by Maggie Wells

Copyright © 2016 by Abdo Consulting Group, Inc.

Published by EPIC Press™
PO Box 398166
Minneapolis, MN 55439

All rights reserved.

Printed in the United States of America.

International copyrights reserved in all countries.
No part of this book may be reproduced in any form without
written permission from the publisher. EPIC Press™ is trademark
and logo of Abdo Consulting Group, Inc.

Cover design by Candice Keimig
Images for cover art obtained from iStockPhoto.com
Edited by Lisa Owens

LIBRARY OF CONGRESS CATALOGING-IN-PUBLICATION DATA

Wells, Maggie.
Jasmine / Maggie Wells.
p. cm. — (Nine months; #3)
Summary: Jasmine is a 19-year-old college freshman—and a professional dancer in
Las Vegas. After an unfortunate incident at a cast party, she finds herself pregnant
forcing her to acknowledge that she can't take care of her daughter and gives her up
for adoption. She then returns home to New Jersey in defeat but ultimately finds
herself back on her feet and self-sufficient, determined to get her daughter back.
ISBN 978-1-68076-192-4 (hardcover)
1. Teenagers—Sexual behavior—Fiction. 2. Teenage pregnancy—Fiction.
3. Sex—Fiction. 4. Adoption—Fiction. 5. Young adult fiction. I. Title.
[Fic]—dc23
2015949412

EPICPRESS.COM

To Joel Hinman

One

IT STARTED LIKE THIS: I WAS WALKING TO CLASS—MANAGERIAL Accounting, if you must know; a dancer can't rely on her body to support her forever, now can she? Anyway, I was running to class, not really walking, because Professor Weed always locked the door as soon as the clock ticked the hour. So, here I was running down the hallway at the University of Nevada, Las Vegas, and with each footfall I was thinking: glutes, core, glutes, core, and it must have been destiny; a flyer printed on pretty pink paper blew off the wall and landed at my feet. All I saw was:

Casting Call: Dancers Wanted.

So I snatched it up and dashed into the classroom just as Weed was closing the door.

"Jasmine, late again?"

You know I wasn't the only one. There were three guys shoving through the door behind me. Why did creepy Weed always single me out? How many times had I explained to him that I have Dance Studio right before his class, and it was halfway across the campus?

As Weed droned on about Full Costing Methods, I slipped the pink paper out of my bag and spread it out on my textbook and smoothed out the creases.

Bally's Hotel & Casino is casting for its long-running dance spectacular, Bacchanal! Seeking male and female singers and dancers to join the cast of the longest-running show in Las Vegas!

Please God, let this be my break! Auditions ended at four—fuck! I wondered if I could make it after my Communications class. Or should I skip class? Decisions, decisions. I really didn't hear anything Weed said that day. I was hoping it didn't show up on the test.

Okay, I skipped my last class, so sue me. Professor Jinks liked me and she was an easy grader anyway. So I got to Bally's and shit, there were a lot of girls there. Big girls, lots of leg, lots of tit (probably fake). How would I ever stand out? First I heard Mom's voice in my head—"You'll never make it"—and then Grandma's voice drowned her out—"Believe in yourself, girl." *Okay, I can do this*, I thought.

"Jasmine, hi!"

I spun around to see Sandra from my Communications class.

"Busted!" I said.

Hey, if she's here, too, I don't feel so bad, I thought.

"What do you think?" she said. "About the competition?"

"Fuck the competition!" We both laughed.

"Here's the director," she whispered. "Eddie Watson."

"Who?"

"Shhh," she shushed me.

The director strode toward us, a black dude, and so young! In sneakers, tight jeans and a mock turtle. Shit, he was hot!

"Hello, ladies!" he shouted. "Anybody who knows me knows that I love dancers. I want to create something so great that people start thinking, 'Wow, those dancers are really amazing.' Now show me what you got."

As we took our positions and the music started, I thanked the Lord that Sandra was with me, shoulder-to-shoulder, hip-to-hip. But with each kick, each shimmy, I gained confidence, enough to smile, to make eye contact. And he was watching me. Wow! He was watching me. Me! At this point, I was channeling Beyoncé. I was owning it. *This is mine!* I thought. *Fuck you, Sandra; see you in Communications class.*

//

Eddie. Was that his name, seriously? How old was he, like eight? Eddie kept his eye on me through the whole first exercise. I know that for a fact because I kept my eye on him the whole time. Then at the break, after he had dismissed half of the girls, including Sandra (sorry, babe!), he singled me out. Jazz, he called me.

"Jazz, trade places with Jules."

I moved up to the center of the front row.

"Let's take it from the top," he called out.

I watched him watching me and I danced for him alone. Each kick, each spin, was bigger, tighter than the last. I had never danced better and I realized at that moment that I needed him and his critical eye of perfection to reach my highest level of achievement. I admit it, I started fantasizing about the power couple we could become. I would be his muse; he would be my Svengali. Wait! Was that a negative thing? Maybe Kanye was a better role model—I could be his Kim. Yes, that was exactly what was going through my head during the audition.

This went on for over an hour—until we were all drenched in sweat, our muscles trembling with fatigue, our faces frozen into smiling grimaces. Finally Eddie called out, "That's it for today, ladies. We'll be sending out callbacks tomorrow. Keep an eye on your phones. I didn't have to say that, now did I?" Eddie laughed at his own joke. I mopped my face with a towel as I watched him prance across the stage, draping his scarf theatrically around his throat. He was immediately engulfed in a cloud of assistants and stage personnel who hung on his every word and gesture.

///

When you have a dream and the talent to match, you have an obligation to the universe to hitch a ride on that star and ride it as far as you can. Mom had never been supportive of my move to

Las Vegas. Yes, she had humored me by enrolling me in dance classes from the age of five, and drove me to dance practice after school every day for years and attended all of my shows and recitals. But, I think she always saw me as an also-ran. She acknowledged that I was good enough to be in the show, but she never believed I could be the star.

"You'll never make a living as a dancer," she had said.

She might have been right about trying to make it on Broadway, but Las Vegas was one of the few places where a dancer could make a decent living. The shows ran for years. You could dance until you were forty. I'd heard of women putting their kids through college on their showgirl paychecks.

//

Back to reality. I should have stretched after the audition, but I was afraid of looking like a wannabe. So, instead, I swaddled myself in sweats and leg warmers and trudged back to campus and across the quad to the library.

I found a carousel on the lower level and spread out my textbook and worksheets. I muted my phone and tucked it into my pocket since Eddie had said we wouldn't hear anything until the next day. I was deep in calculations on the present value of a stream of projected cash flow when my pocket began to buzz. I ignored it, thinking it was from one of my study buddies, but the buzzing wouldn't stop. I dug the phone out of my pocket and saw a bunch of green message icons in my text feed.

Please confirm

Please confirm

Please confirm

Please confirm

I swiped to unlock my phone and scrolled through the messages.

Congratulations! You passed the first round of the audition process for Bacchanal. The next round is scheduled for 2 p.m. tomorrow.

I clicked to confirm and slammed my book shut. Priorities! Accounting could wait—I shoved everything into my bag and ran to the dance studio to stretch and grab a sauna before collapsing into bed.

Two

Hi Professor,
   I woke up this morning with a high fever and won't be able to make it to class. Is the lecture available online?
   Thanks,
   Jasmine.

Okay, I know I should have gone to class. But I was too excited, too distracted, too focused. I spent the morning in the studio, warming up. I drank a protein smoothie for lunch and then headed over to the audition.

This time, there were only ten girls. *Bacchanal*

was a big show with dozens of dancers; we must have been auditioning for a handful of openings—probably high up in the back. None of that mattered to me. I was feeling good, strong, empowered by the spotlight.

We took our positions and I eyed the competition. Surrounded by blondes, and one enormous redhead, I was probably the smallest and definitely the only dark-skinned girl in the line. What look were they going for? I guess I could look at this two ways: either I didn't have a shot in hell, or I would stand out in the line-up. I decided to go with the second theory and threw myself into the audition, heart and soul.

But by the first break, I was pretty discouraged. Eddie hadn't been looking at me much at all. He kept calling out to the redhead—Ginger, he called her, although I'm pretty sure her name was Joanne.

"More hip, Ginger!" he said. "Bigger arch. Good girl!"

At the break, Ginger stood off to the side of the studio, nursing a bottle of water. I wandered over.

"Eddie seems to really like you," I said, hoping that didn't sound like I was jealous or anything. Hell, yeah, I was jealous.

"I don't know about that," she said. "I think maybe he thinks I'm too old and he's just pushing me to see if I have the stamina."

Close up, I realized that Ginger must have been over thirty.

"You've been dancing for a long time?" I asked.

"Since I was your age, kid," she said. "What are you—eighteen?"

"Nineteen," I replied.

"You in school?" Ginger asked.

"I'm a sophomore at UNLV," I said. "But this is my dream. What do you think my chances are?"

"Oh, I think you're already hired," Ginger said. "I heard that they're adding a second show. Whoops—there's the buzzer. Break time is over. Nice to meet you, Jazz."

"Jasmine," I said.

"I think you're Jazz from now on," Ginger said. "You'll need a stage name if you want to hold on to some anonymity. You don't want creeps showing up at your door in the middle of the night."

As I walked back toward the lineup, I wondered what she had meant by that. I'd always planned to build my dancer's profile on the Internet Broadway Database online. I would need to use my real name if I wanted to get work on Broadway.

We lined up shoulder-to-shoulder, backs arched, poised as we waited for Eddie to enter the stage. He walked gracefully and deliberately along the line, appraising each girl with a languorous gaze, as if he were undressing each of us with his eyes. He doubled back and came to stand at the center.

"Ladies," he said. "I'm sure by now you've all heard the exciting news. The producers are backing a second show of *Bacchanal*. We'll be performing five nights a week at ten o'clock. We're developing an authentic old-Vegas style show. I think you know what I'm talking about?"

There were some murmurs and gasps along the line.

"What is he talking about?" I whispered to the blonde to my right.

"Full frontal," she hissed back.

"This is purely voluntary," Eddie said. "I'm looking for volunteers. Mostly just topless, perhaps a hint of a little more—we need to keep the audience guessing, and the morality board at bay. And of course, we're offering combat pay."

"What's combat pay?" I whispered to the blonde to my left.

"Thirty percent bonus," she muttered. "You could make more as a stripper down the street."

"Any volunteers?" Eddie asked. "Please step forward."

I was suddenly aware that there was a bunch of stagehands standing off in the wings, staring. But, seeing this as my big break and a way to guarantee my spot in the show, I took a giant step forward. I think I saw a couple of other girls farther down the line step up as well. I held my breath.

"Jazz?" Eddie asked.

Oh, shit, I thought, he doesn't mean me. He doesn't want a black girl. I started to step back.

"Show us what you got, baby," Eddie said.

Aware of the leering eyes of the stagehands, I slipped my leotard off my shoulders and pulled it down off of my breasts. Not sure what he wanted to see, I stopped at my hipbones, my fingers still hooked in the spandex.

"That's enough," Eddie said. "You can save the rest for later. Turn to the left."

I did, thinking, *Fuck you assholes. Are you getting an eyeful?*

"Turn to the right," Eddie said.

I narrowed my eyes and steeled myself against any emotion.

"Okay, next." Eddie had moved down the line.

I pulled up my leotard and slipped back into the line. I held myself erect and stared straight into space for what seemed like forever.

"Okay, Ladies," Eddie called out. "Rehearsals start on Monday at four. See Marcus in HR to get your paperwork together for payroll."

That was it—I was in! I was officially a professional dancer. I couldn't wait to call Mom and say *I told you so!* All those years of trying to dampen my ambitions. *Life doesn't always hand you lemons, Mom!* I went to grab my towel and bottle of water and was heading for the dressing room when I heard my name.

"Jazz, a moment?" It was Tommy, one of Eddie's assistants. "Eddie wants to speak with you. In his office. Follow me."

///

Aware that I was drenched in sweat and probably stunk to high hell, I mopped my pits and wrapped my towel around my neck before I followed Tommy down the hall backstage.

Tommy tapped on the door with his knuckles and cracked it open. "I have Jazz," he said.

Tommy pushed the door open. Eddie was sprawled on a sofa covered in floral chintz. That's a word Mom would have used. Chintz. I'm not even sure what it meant. Was this the infamous casting couch? I had heard rumors about Eddie hitting on girls who worked for him and I was wary.

"Sit down." Eddie gestured toward a chair.

I did.

"Jazz," Eddie said. "You opened my eyes."

"Really?" I asked. Oh no, where was this going?

"No, really," he said. "Exotic. That's what this show needs. I'm going to pitch the producers on an exotic, erotic element. I need to find a few more girls to back you up—maybe Asian—can we find one with big tits? Maybe Spanish or Caribbean. But you're the headliner; you're my muse. I'm going to create a dance number just for you."

"Let's set up some time in the studio to choreograph some moves," Eddie said. "Tomorrow, okay?"

"I have class," I said. "I'll be done at two forty."

"Class?" Eddie said. "Are you fucking kidding me? I just offered you headliner—your name on the marquee. Tourists will come from all over the world to see Jazz in *Bacchanal*."

Tommy interrupted. "Eddie, you are booked solid until three tomorrow."

Eddie glowered at Tommy. "Okay, fuck it. Meet me here at three."

To Tommy, he said, "Post the new positions for exotic . . . " He caught himself. "Not exotic dancers—we don't want to attract that element. We're looking for dancers of color—that's the term, right?" Eddie seemed very pleased with himself.

"Thanks, Jazzy, baby," Eddie said. "See you tomorrow at three. This is going to be hot!"

Three

THE SECOND THE CLOCK HIT TWO FORTY, I JUMPED UP and scooped my notebooks into my backpack. I had just reached the door when I heard Sandra call my name.

"You got the callback?" Sandra asked.

"I did," I said. "I got the gig, actually. I'm supposed to be at rehearsal right now. Sorry, but I gotta go."

I felt sorry for Sandra. I remember that feeling—watching the other girls get called back and then walking home, dejected, wondering what it was they had that I didn't. That's what Sandra was thinking—why me and not her?

The rehearsal room was empty when I arrived at three on the dot. I stood by the door for a few minutes, wondering if Eddie had forgotten about me. Then I figured, what the heck, might as well warm up. I adjusted my ear buds and cranked up the volume on my iPod. I got lost in the music and was spinning around the room when I saw Eddie's reflection in the mirror.

I scurried over to where I had dropped my bag and slipped my iPod into it. "How long have you been standing there?" I asked.

"Long enough," he said.

I detected a faint smile, so I figured he wasn't angry. He walked over to the control panel and flicked some switches. Music flooded the room.

"Now, let's do this my way," he said.

He led me to the center of the room and stood behind me facing the mirror. He placed one hand on my right hip and with other stretched my left arm up over my head. As he counted out the beats he walked me through the routine. We danced together for over two hours, until I was breathless and soaked in sweat.

"That's it," he said at last. "Let's meet again tomorrow before rehearsal. Like four o'clock?"

"Sure," I said. *Did I do okay?* I wondered.

I bundled up in my sweats and was about to leave.

"Jazz," he said. "You are my muse, baby. We are going to rock this town."

//

His words rang in my head as I crossed the parking lot to my car. The autumn sun hung swollen and red, just glancing off the mountains in the distance. I had never felt so in love before, in love with myself, with life, with the universe, and every living thing. I wanted to call somebody, but who? Not Mom, she wouldn't understand what I was feeling. Life was one big disappointment to her; she wouldn't be happy for me. I hadn't made any close friends at school; I didn't really know anybody in town. At that moment, I made a vow to change that—meet people, make a friend. *Maybe I'll find a friend in the show*, I thought.

///

As I pulled into the parking lot of my apartment building, my neighbor, Mrs. Meacham, was unloading bags of groceries from her trunk. Mrs. Meacham was a retired schoolteacher in her late sixties. Her daughter had moved to Los Angeles and she was living alone.

"Mrs. Meacham!" I called out. "Let me help you."

As we climbed the stairs to the second floor apartments, Mrs. Meacham asked, "Are you just getting home from school?" She knew I was a student at UNLV.

"Actually, I've had the most amazing day," I said.

"Well, isn't that wonderful," she said as she unlocked her apartment door. "Would you like to stay for dinner?"

"Sure," I said. "As long as you let me help with the cooking." Grateful for the audience, I poured my story out as I unpacked the groceries and boiled the pasta.

"Does this mean you'll be dropping out of school?" Mrs. Meacham asked.

"Hell, no!" I said. "Sorry. It's just that my mom never finished college. Ever since I was little, I knew that I had to go to college and learn about business so I wouldn't end up driving a bus like her. But being a dancer is like being an athlete. I know I won't be able to dance forever. I need to figure out how to make a business out of it."

"Smart cookie," Mrs. Meacham said.

///

"Mom, you're not going to believe it," I said into the phone. "I made it! I'm in the show. Five nights a week. I'm making enough money to pay rent and tuition—no more student loans!"

"Wait until I tell your Grandma!" Mom said. "She never believed in you. But I did, didn't I? When does it open? We'll come out for a visit, Grandma and me."

"Um," I said. Oh shit! I never thought Mom would actually come to Vegas to see me dance.

"We'll do a little gambling, a little shopping." Mom was still talking. "It's been too long since we took a vacation. And Grandma misses you."

"It's too early, Mom," I lied. "Eddie—that's the director—he's still making changes. I'll call you when everything is ready. Bye, Mom."

///

Somehow Eddie had found five other dark-skinned dancers to back me up. Some days I wondered whether we were being exploited—the black chicks were the naked ones on stage—but on other days I felt so grateful for the opportunity to make some money and pay down my debt, while doing what I loved.

We rehearsed every day for five hours, finally quitting at nine thirty p.m. Then I drove my ten-year-old Miata the two miles back to my one-bedroom apartment at South Cove. I lived on the second floor overlooking the pool. Generally, the place was pretty quiet except for the occasional drunken pool party—then the howls and crash of glass meeting cement would echo in the courtyard, making it hard to concentrate on my homework.

I was late to class on more than one occasion. Professor Weed seemed to be keeping an eye out for me and would unlock the door as I approached.

As usual, there were one or two guys sliding in right behind me.

One day, as he called my name for roll call, Professor Weed said, "See me after class."

There was a line of students waiting to talk to Weed. I hung back and waited until they were gone.

"You wanted to speak to me?" I asked.

"Jasmine, your grade on the last test was quite disappointing," he said. "Not up to your usual standard. You haven't taken advantage of my office hours. Is there anything going on? Anything I can help you with?"

Pervy Weed, I thought. *That's what you want—to get me alone in your office.*

"I'm sorry, Professor Weed," I said. "It's my job—I've been working nights to pay for my rent and tuition."

"Can you cut back on your hours?" Weed asked. "Maybe a little more time to focus on your studies?"

"No," I said. Oh, hell, tell him the truth, she thought. "I'm dancing in a show on the Strip. We're opening next week and I have to be there from eight to twelve, five nights a week. We're off on Mondays and Fridays. I promise I'll catch up."

"I see." Weed shuffled through papers for a long minute and then looked up.

"Jasmine," he said at last. "I'm sure this is a great opportunity for you. Clearly, you are a talented dancer. But you need to make a choice. I would recommend that you focus on your schoolwork right now. Finish your degree and then dance for a few years. Dancing is the kind of career that won't last that long. Five, maybe ten years if you are lucky. Your degree in accounting will last you a lifetime."

"I'm sure you know this," Weed said, "but grades matter to get a good job with a top accounting firm, or even in a corporate accounting department. They're looking for A students. I know you have the potential. I don't want to see it go to waste."

Maybe Weed wasn't such a perv after all? Maybe he actually saw me as a gifted student? Maybe I was just exhausted, but I started to tear up. I was under a lot of pressure.

"I'm sorry, Professor Weed. I truly am. I appreciate your faith in me. I really want this. And I will make it up to you."

Four

ONCE THE SHOW OPENED, THINGS SEEMED TO FALL INTO place. We performed Tuesday, Wednesday, Thursday, Saturday, and Sunday at ten p.m. Stage call was at eight, and I was in bed by one a.m. I spent my afternoons at the library and wrote a couple of extra papers to improve my grades. I was feeling pretty good about things.

Eddie had lied about putting my name on the marquee. Instead they added the words "Exotic, Erotic" and the silhouette—a caricature, really— of a black woman. That was probably better, anyway. Ginger's warning about maintaining my anonymity came to mind every time I returned home to find a rowdy pool party going on. The whistles and catcalls were bad enough without them thinking that I was working as a stripper. And I certainly didn't want Mom Googling *Bacchanal* and stumbling upon illicit videos. The ones on the Bally's website were bad enough, even though it looked like they were shot slightly out of focus.

But all in all, I was pretty proud of myself. I was dancing in a hit show, earning combat pay, and maintaining an A- average. I felt like I had really hit my stride.

//

The show had been running for several weeks, and the late show was a sell-out every night. It was a Thursday night and the dressing room was buzzing about a Christmas party at Eddie's house.

"Are you going?" my friend Katrina asked.

Katrina was a big Swedish blonde, in her thirties; she stood at least six feet in heels. She spoke with a bit of a lilt—she was from Minnesota I think.

"I don't have anything to wear," I said. "All I have are my sweats."

"You should keep a dress and heels in your bag," Katrina said. "You never know when it might be date night."

"Date night!" I said. "I haven't had a date in two years."

"Maybe if you didn't walk around in sweats all the time," Katrina said, laughing.

"Who has time?" I asked. "I can't even imagine trying to fit a boyfriend into my life right now."

"Who's talking about a boyfriend?" Katrina said.

//

I was heading to the stage door when Eddie came around the corner. He was dressed in his usual getup: black jeans, mock turtle, and expensive-looking Italian leather jacket.

"Jazz!" he said. "I've been looking for you everywhere."

Really, where had he looked?

"Big party at my place tonight—can I give you a ride?"

I felt like such a slob in my sweats and Uggs. "Um," I said. "I'd love to, but I can't go like this."

"No," he said, "Of course not. Go to Rousso's shop in the mall—use my house account." Eddie pulled out his phone and texted the shop to say that Jasmine was on her way.

"Eddie, what are you doing?"

"It's done," Eddie said. "The girl is expecting you. Get yourself something pretty. Something sparkly. It's Christmas!"

"Eddie, I can't accept this," I said.

"It's Christmas," he repeated.

///

Okay, it's Christmas; my boss sent me shopping as a Christmas gift. As creepy as it seemed that Eddie had a house account at a women's dress shop in Bally's, I couldn't resist the urge to splurge. Every day as I walked past the fancy, high-end shops in the casino and drooled over the dresses in the windows, I fantasized about what it would be like to have money some day. I had always wondered what it would be like to walk in and slap down some plastic and pick out whatever I wanted. Here was my chance! And you know what, I liked it! I didn't care that the shop lady was eyeing me like I was a call girl. I found a hot little number in dusty blue silk, a pair of strappy sandals and some dangly crystal earrings. I felt pretty, and suddenly, I was in the mood to party. I didn't want to think about the possible strings attached, any expectations that Eddie might have.

///

In front of Eddie's place, I parked my Miata next to someone's Bentley. Whatever—nobody told me not to! The house was all lit up and music was coming from the pool area out back. The front door was unlocked and I walked in like I owned the place. I thought, *if only Mom could see me now.* This was a lifestyle that I could get used to. A waiter in a tux approached with a tray of glasses of champagne. I took one and walked down a long, tiled hallway toward the music.

Outside the stars sparkled in the sky and the moonbeams bounced off the ripples in the pool. There were people dancing, laughing, and circulating on the pool deck. A few people had stripped off their clothes and were floating in the pool. I stood by the bar holding my glass, hoping I would recognize someone and they would rescue me. I saw Eddie sitting on the stairs in the shallow end talking to Katrina. When he saw me, he stood up and climbed out of the pool, completely naked.

He was walking toward me. I looked for a place to hide, but it was too late.

"Jazz!" he said. "You came."

I didn't know where to look. "Uh, hi," I said. *Man, this is awkward.*

"Come in the pool," he said. "The water is nice."

I made some feeble excuses—it was a new dress; I had just done my make-up—to no avail. The next thing I knew, he was tugging at the zipper on my dress.

"Eddie!" I cried. "Cut it out. You're getting water on me!"

"My dress, right?" Eddie said. "My store account?"

Just then, I realized what a mistake I had made by accepting the dress. I felt everyone watching as he unzipped my dress and it fell to my ankles. *Sure, I have gotten used to performing topless on stage but here I am* off the clock! *I have boundaries!*

Eddie took my hand and dragged me toward the steps into the pool. He was giving me no choice.

"Wait, my sandals!" *I don't want to ruin these babies*, I thought. I slipped them off and followed him down the steps and into the pool. I just wanted to disappear into the dark water. And you know, he was right. The water was nice. It had been a long week of work and school and my muscles were sore. It felt great to float and gaze up into the night sky. Well, it would have felt better if his hands hadn't been all over me. One minute I felt like a million bucks in my pretty silk dress and heels. The next I was just a piece of meat being manhandled by a brute. He was pulling at my panties and groping my vagina.

"Eddie!" I cried. "Cut it out." I pushed his hands away.

"What's the matter, baby?" he asked, grabbing my arm. "Just lie back and relax. Look up. Enjoy the stars."

"I think I need to get out of the pool," I said. I pushed him away and swam toward the ladder.

"Jazz," he said. "Come back. I promise I won't touch you."

I clung to the ladder and thought, *what do I do now? I need a towel or a robe. Why did I get into the pool? How do I get out of here gracefully?*

A waiter walked by.

"Do you have towels?" I asked.

"No ma'am," he said. "Just drinks."

He offered me a glass of champagne and I took it and downed it, still clinging to the ladder. My head was starting to spin.

Suddenly, Eddie was right behind me.

"Jazz, baby," he said. "Don't go. The water is nice, isn't it?"

Oh, God, please get away from me, I thought. "I'd like to get out. Are there any towels?"

"Let me get you another drink," he said. "Relax. Everything is okay."

I don't remember anything else that night.

Five

I WOKE UP IN A STRANGE BED, NAKED. I PRESSED MY hands to my eyes to block out the bright sun and racked my brain. *Where am I? How did I get here?* Slowly the memories came back—the show, the dress, the party, and the pool. *I must still be at Eddie's house,* I thought. *But where are my clothes?* I got up and found the bathroom. There was a pink (!) robe hanging on the back of the door. I slipped it on and washed my face and tried to fluff up my hair. *Where are my clothes?* I wondered again. *Where is my bag? Please tell me nothing happened last night!* But I felt sore and bruised and I feared the worst. *Maybe I slipped and fell? I hope I didn't embarrass myself last night.* All I could think was that I wanted to go home and climb into bed and block the whole night out of my memory.

I poked my head outside of the bedroom door and smelled coffee. I tiptoed downstairs and there was Eddie, standing in the kitchen in a white terrycloth robe with his back to me. He turned around.

"Good morning!" he said.

"What happened?" I asked. "Where are my clothes?"

"You had a little too much champagne last night," he said. "I tucked you into bed. Your clothes are on the sofa." He pointed toward the living room. "Everything is cool. Do you want some coffee? A bagel?"

Everything is cool? What is that supposed to mean? My head was pounding and I ached all over. I needed to put something in my stomach. "A bagel would be great."

Eddie had set the table out by the pool. I dug

my sunglasses out of my bag and walked outside. The warmth of the sun soothed my throbbing temples. *What day is it?*

Eddie brought out a tray. "How do you like your coffee?" he asked.

"Black, please," I said.

We ate in silence for a few minutes.

"Why did you put me to bed naked?" I asked.

"You fell asleep in the pool," he said. "What was I going to do, try to put your clothes back on?"

"I don't get it," I said. "I only had one glass of champagne—maybe two."

He didn't say anything.

"What day is this?" I asked. "Do we have a curtain call at eight?"

"No," he said. "It's Friday. We're off until tomorrow."

"Oh, good," I said. I felt stupid for not knowing that it was Friday. I finished the bagel and took a couple of sips of coffee. "I guess I'll go then."

I gathered my clothes and dressed in the powder room. I could only find one earring. I was bummed—I really liked those earrings. But I didn't want to go fishing around upstairs—God only knows what I'd find—some other girl's earring, I suppose. I hung the robe on the back of the door. I wondered, briefly, to whom it belonged, but then quickly dismissed the thought. I wanted to flush the whole night from my memory bank. I hadn't been fired, as far as I could tell. I wanted to leave on a high note.

"Thanks Eddie," I said as I opened the door. "Nice party."

He didn't say anything.

//

Right after Christmas, Eddie disappeared. The rumor I heard was that he was in L.A. working with Beyoncé on her new tour. Geri, his lead assistant, took over.

January kicked off convention season and the show was sold out through April. Maybe it was the pressure of starting a new semester or maybe the routine of school, library, the Strip, and home to crash had caught up with me, but something wasn't right. I didn't have my usual level of energy; I felt heavy and sluggish. It got harder each day to get out of bed in the morning and I had taken to napping in the library.

The first time I stumbled on stage, nobody seemed to notice. Then it happened a second time, and Katrina caught my arm to steady me.

"Are you okay?" she whispered.

I nodded, but I wasn't so sure.

//

That night, after the show, Katrina approached me in the dressing room.

"Are you sure you're okay?" she said. "You look tired."

I looked at Katrina warily. Had Eddie said something to her about me after the party? Did she know that I had woken up in his bed? Did everybody know?

"I'm exhausted," I said. "Maybe I'll take a week off—go home for spring break."

///

As the plane circled over Newark airport, I had never felt so happy to see the Manhattan skyline in the distance. I reminded myself that I was living my dream—I was a professional dancer— why did I suddenly feel like I just wanted to move back home? I told myself, *you're just tired.* Going to school and working full-time would tire anyone out. Maybe I should cut back on my class schedule? Or take a semester off? But the show was slated to run for years and I didn't want to put off college indefinitely. No, better to graduate on schedule and then things would get easier.

//

The Uber driver was waiting for me curbside.

"Coming in from Vegas?" he asked. I could see his eyes trained on me in the rearview mirror. "What's in Vegas?"

"Work," I said. I hesitated and then I added, "and school." That's the first time I had answered the question by saying "work." And I said work before school. I was pondering that, thinking about my priorities, and I didn't hear his next question.

"I'm sorry?" I asked.

"I asked what kind of work you do in Vegas?" he asked. "You work in the casinos?"

"I'm a dancer," I said.

"A showgirl?" His eyes lit up. "In a titty show?"

I looked out the window but all I could see was

my reflection and the dark circles under my tired eyes.

//

"This is me," I said. The driver pulled up in front of Mom's house and jumped out to help me with my roller bag. Mom opened the door and stood silhouetted in the doorway.

"Mom!" I started crying as I dragged my bag up the walk to the front door.

Inside, she looked at me hard. "Jasmine, you do not look well," Mom said.

"I'm just tired, Mom," I said. "I'm going to go crawl into bed and we can talk in the morning, okay?"

//

The next morning, I woke up with a migraine. I buried my head in the pillows and tried to shut out the light.

"What is up with your lazy ass?" Mom shouted through the door.

"I don't feel well," I said. I moaned and rolled over.

"Do I need to call the doctor?" Mom asked.

"I think so," I said.

Six

"STEP ONTO THE SCALE," NURSE DRAKE SAID. SHE SHIFTED the sliding weight back and forth for way too long. "One twenty-five," she finally said.

"What?" I gasped. I had never weighed more than one hundred and twenty pounds in my life, and before Christmas, with all the extra activity between rehearsals and performances, I had been down to one hundred and five.

"What's your normal weight?" Nurse Drake asked.

"One ten, one fifteen," I said.

"Hmm," she said. "When was your last period?"

"I'm a dancer," I said. "I've never been very regular."

"Did you leave a urine sample?" she asked.

"Yes," I replied.

"Hmm," she said again. "Let's hop up on the table and the doctor will see you in a moment."

I sat on the table in a paper robe, swinging my legs back and forth, back and forth, thinking. I had never had to watch my diet; if anything I saw food as fuel to keep me at my peak performance. What was I doing wrong? I was mulling this over in my head when I heard a tap on the door.

"Hi, I'm Dr. Arrington." She was stylishly coiffed with designer glasses, spike heels and a tailored suit under her white coat. She settled into her chair and looked over my chart. "What's going on?" she asked.

"I don't know what's wrong with me," I said. "I'm tired all the time. I'm putting on weight for no reason. I make my living as a dancer. I need to get back in shape, fast."

"You're a dancer?" Dr. Arrington asked. "Ballet, Broadway—where do you work?"

"I'm a showgirl in Las Vegas," I said. "I work at Bally's."

"Exciting!" she said. She flipped a couple pages on my chart and looked up over the rim of her glasses. "Ms. Walker? Did you know that you're pregnant?"

"What?" I gasped. "How can that be?"

"Are you sexually active?" Dr. Arrington asked.

"No!" I said. "I haven't had a date in almost two years."

"Really?" Dr. Arrington asked. "No sexual activity?"

I buried my face in my hands. *Eddie! The Christmas party! Waking up naked in his bed? Please! How stupid could I be?*

Tears streamed down my face. "I think I was raped," I said. "I went to a party at my boss's house and I woke up naked in his bed and I don't remember anything that happened that night."

Dr. Arrington took my hand. "I know this is

a lot of information to process right now, but we have options here. There are rape crisis counselors on call, you can report the incident to the police; we can schedule you for an abortion. We've already tested you for STDs and I will call you with those results. Tell me what you want to do."

"I want to go home," I said.

"Of course," Dr. Arrington said. "Let me give you my card. Here's my cell. You can call me anytime."

How did I let this happen? How could I have been so stupid? Eddie always struck me as a predatory creep—why did I go to his party? Why did I accept a second drink? Why didn't I just get out of the pool, grab my dress and run into the house?

//

Mom took one look at my face and knew something was wrong. She waited until we were in the car.

"What did the doctor say?" she asked.

"You're not going to believe it," I said. "I can't even believe it. I'm pregnant."

Mom let out a huge sigh. "How did this happen?" she asked. "Don't answer that!"

"Mom!" I said.

"You haven't told me," she said. "Do you have a boyfriend?"

"No, Mom, I don't have a boyfriend. I'm not sure exactly what happened, but I went to a party at Eddie's house. The director? Eddie? I woke up the next morning in his bed. I'm not saying that he did it, but I don't remember anything that happened that night."

"You got drunk at a party and your boss took advantage of you?" Mom asked. "I guess you got what you were asking for."

"Mom!"

"You need to call that man," Mom said. "He needs to step up, here. He's not knocking up no daughter of mine!"

Knocked up! This is a nightmare; please tell me that I'm dreaming. What about the show? What about my career? I can't have a baby. This will ruin my whole life!

"I'll get an abortion," I said. "I need to get back to school and work. I can't do this." I knew that wasn't really an option. Mom was a devout Baptist and had dragged me to the protests her church organized at Planned Parenthood clinics for as long as I could remember. She would have disowned me.

"Oh no you will not!" Mom said. "I did not raise you to kill an unborn child. That man has money. You're going to call him and tell him to pay up."

"But what about the show?" I sobbed. *I want to be a dancer. This can't be happening!*

"Forget about the damn show," Mom said. "They are going to fire your ass anyway. Soon as they find out."

So I called Eddie and got his voice mail. I left a message. Seventeen times. The week went by.

//

"He's not answering, and he's not returning my calls," I said.

"Maybe he'll be in Vegas when you get back?" Mom suggested.

"Maybe." I said. "What if he doesn't want to have anything to do with me or the baby?"

"We'll get a paternity test," Mom said. "We'll force him to stand up and be a man."

//

But of course, Eddie wasn't there when I got back. I tried to jump back into my school and work routine but I was definitely not on my game. I couldn't keep up with the music and kept flubbing my pivots. Therefore, it didn't come as much of a surprise when Geri pulled me aside a week later and told me that she had to let me go.

"I'm sorry, doll," she said. "Eddie built this show around you, you know. Give us a call when you're feeling better and we'll see what we can do."

Seven

U P UNTIL THE MINUTE THAT GERI FIRED ME, I THINK I WAS in denial. I didn't remember anything from that night, wanting to believe it had never really happened. And because she left the door open to return when I "felt better," I didn't believe my career was over, either. Somehow I convinced myself that I could do it all—be a successful dancer and a mother. A lot of the dancers in the show had kids, why not me?

//

So that's what happened. The next few months were a blur. I want to tell you that I loved being pregnant, that I was glowing and felt at one with the universe and my womanhood. Bullshit! I was fucking miserable. First it was the headaches, then the vomiting, and then the backaches and shortness of breath. I was uncomfortable and cranky all of the time. I had a theory about this. Those earth-mother types who celebrate pregnancy and ripen with every stage—those bitches aren't for real. I obsessed over ads that featured girls in bikinis. I desperately wanted to have a waist again. And most of all, I wanted this thing out of me. Like an alien invasion it had taken over my body, my hormones and even my brain. I wanted my life back!

To make matters worse, money was tight. I ran through my savings and I couldn't apply for financial aid again until August, so things got pretty lean by May.

"I'm sorry to ask again," I said to Mom on the phone.

"Money is tight here too, you know," Mom said. "The transit union hasn't renewed our contract but okay, I'll make a transfer. And school is out soon, right? Can you come home for the summer? It must be hotter than Hades there."

"No, Mom. I'll find a job," I said. "I've been applying online. I have a few interviews this week—bookkeeper, admin, waitress—that kind of thing. I'll pay you back as soon as I can."

///

The first interview was at the Peppermill Diner. It was an original—from the seventies—and big with the tourist/convention crowd. They hired a lot of ex-showgirls—that was part of the mystique. Katrina had gotten me the interview with Perry, the assistant manager.

I picked up a little number from A Pea in the Pod. It was flattering and didn't scream maternity. I thought that I could pass for pleasantly plump.

I checked in with the hostess and told her I had

an interview with Perry. She told me to wait in a booth. I practiced my story in my head. I used to be a showgirl, but I quit to focus on school full-time. I'm hard working, a self-starter—what were the other buzzwords that they wanted to hear?

Perry turned out to be a short, round Jewish guy with a full head of fluffy, silver hair. At first he was all smiles but then he channeled his inner prosecutor.

"Jasmine, is it?" He looked at my application. "You look a little young to be an ex-showgirl. My girls," he gestured around the room. "They're over forty, maybe fifty. What gives?"

"No, I am," I stammered. "I was in *Bacchanal*—you know the show at Bally's? But, I'm also going to school and I decided to focus on finishing up school. The long hours were too much for me—but I'll go back once I graduate."

"So, you're a short-timer, then?" he asked. "I get you for a year? And then you quit?"

"Two years," I said. "I have two years of school

to go. I can commit to working here for two years."

How had this conversation gone so awry? He had painted me into a corner. I think I said I would waitress for two years and then dance for ten years and return to waitressing? What, you can't be an ex-showgirl who only danced for six months?

"Look," I said. "I really need this job, and I'll work hard and I'm reliable and a self-starter. Give me a shot. If, after a month, I'm not the best waitress in here, you can fire me. I'll work my ass off, I promise you."

After a long pause, he finally spoke. "Jasmine, I have to be honest with you. The tourists, they come here to see my girls. The service might not be the best; the food is just so-so. You see these girls—they're not young, but they keep their bodies in shape. It's a fantasyland. I'm not sure you're a fit."

He'd been so careful to sidestep the words fat

or pregnant. Not that I'd sue him anyway, but his meaning was obvious.

As soon as I got to my car, the tears flowed. I couldn't even get a crappy waitressing job?

Interview number two was for a receptionist position at a shipping company. I wore the same outfit but this time with conservative pumps and minimal makeup. The office was in one of those low-slung office parks that are just a series of corrugated steel garage doors. Navis Pack & Ship was located in Bay 43B. The whole situation looked pretty dubious and I felt way overdressed, but I was desperate for a job.

The garage door was open, so I poked my head inside.

"Hello?" I called out. "I'm looking for Marge?"

A burly man in coveralls stepped out, wiping his hands on a greasy rag. "Who are you?"

"I'm here for the admin position?" I said, uncertain.

"Marge stepped out," he said. "She'll be back soon. Do you want to sit down?"

I followed him inside the garage bay to a tiny, glassed-in office. "You can wait in here."

The office was airless. There was an A/C unit in the wall that made a loud groaning noise but didn't seem to blow any cold air. I started to sweat. I tried to imagine coming to work here every morning in shorts and a baggy T-shirt to sit at this little desk and process orders and invoices.

Just then, Marge walked in. "Jasmine, right?" She held out her hand. "Hi, Doll!" she said. She arranged herself behind the desk.

"So here's the gist of it," she said. "You need to open the mail and make copies of everything. Enter everything into the system and file them in the filing cabinet behind you. Answer the phone— and if any orders come in, you need to fill out the paperwork and enter the information into the computer. How does that sound?"

"Sounds good," I said. "It sounds pretty easy."

"It's a very fast-paced environment," Marge said. "Do you think you can handle it? Doing three things at once?"

"That sounds exciting," I said. And it did. Maybe I had underestimated this gig.

"So," Marge said. "I'm not supposed to technically ask this question but, are you pregnant? Because you look like you're pregnant. I'm only asking because we're looking for someone long-term and if you need to leave for maternity reasons, maybe you're not such a good fit."

Here we go again, I thought. These crappy minimum wage jobs—are they seriously looking for someone to make a long-term commitment?

"Ms. Marge," I said. "I really want this job. Can you give me a chance to prove myself?"

But she had already made up her mind. I guess the line of applicants was longer than I thought.

"Thank you for your time," Marge said. "We'll be in touch."

Interview number three was for a bookkeeper at a busy dental practice. This time I brought my transcript and had highlighted my As in accounting. I checked in with the receptionist.

"I'm here to see Mrs. Patterson," I said.

"Have a seat, dear. She'll be back from lunch in a few minutes."

The waiting room was crowded and noisy. A man and his wife were bickering over a misplaced insurance card. A brother and sister were playing tug-of-war with a coloring book. She hit him and he screamed, "Mom!" I found an empty spot— the chair was hard and uncomfortable. I suddenly needed to pee.

The waiting room door swung open and a pregnant woman walked in. She entered the inner office and greeted the receptionist, who then gestured in my direction.

Please God, don't let that be Mrs. Patterson, I

thought. But of course it was. And wouldn't you know it Mrs. Patterson was looking for someone to fill in during her maternity leave. Except she was due one month before I was, so there you have it. Bad luck, bad timing, whatever you wanted to call it—I felt like the whole universe was stacked against me.

//

I sat in my car in the parking lot and pounded the steering wheel. *Fuck, fuck, fuck!* I drove slowly home, feeling completely defeated. Just as I was pulling into the parking lot, I saw the sign at the car wash next door.

"Help Wanted: Cashier."

I went upstairs and changed into cut-offs and a baggy T-shirt. Now I just looked like a fat black chick, and sure enough, Mr. Fong hired me. He also happened to be my landlord. It turns out he owned every business on the block.

Eight

BY JUNE THE AVERAGE TEMPERATURE WAS NINETY degrees. It would soar to one hundred and five in July. The A/C inside the car wash mini-mart could barely keep up with the customers coming and going; a bell above the door tinkled every time someone entered or exited. It drove me nuts. But at least I had a stool behind the counter. The hours were seven to seven. I waddled home at the end of the day, stripped off my uniform, and plunged into the pool. Sometimes I would float on my back for hours, until the stars came out. My belly was a growing island in the fading light.

I dialed Mom.

"You're out of money already?" Those were her first words.

"No, Mom," I said. "Geez! I found a job."

"You got the bookkeeping gig?" she asked.

"Car wash cashier," I replied. "Hey, it's not so bad. It's right next door to my apartment. I'm clearing five hundred dollars a week and I'm not spending any money on commuting."

"How are you going to stay in school and care for a baby? Explain that to me." She had made me promise to enroll in school as a condition of moving to Las Vegas. I had wanted so badly to make it as a dancer. I wanted to prove to her that I could make it on my own.

"I don't know, Mom. I'll figure something out. How did you manage to have me when you were working full-time?" I asked.

"Your grandma took over," she said. "That's

what you need to do. Come home and your grandma can watch the baby. You can go to school in New Jersey."

I reassured her that everything would be okay. I wanted to believe it was true, but I had made such a mess of everything.

///

The baby. I needed a name. Dr. Finch had told me it was a girl. I spent a lot of time behind the car wash register surfing Facebook on my phone. I typed in a search for "baby names" and came across a page called Nine Months. It was a bunch of pregnant teens, some as young as fifteen! Out of curiosity, I scrolled through the feed.

Aleecia: My baby-daddy says he'll marry me but my mom wants me to get an abortion. She's taking me to Orlando today

Luciana: What's in Orlando?

Aleecia: That's the closest abortion clinic. It's a hundred miles.

Shawna: Don't do it. Do you love your baby-daddy?

Aleecia: I think so

Isabella: You need to be sure. This is your life we're talking about

I decided to jump in.

Jasmine: I need a name for my baby

Candace: I'm calling mine Squirt

Aleecia: What? You can't name a baby Squirt!

Jasmine: I toyed with the idea of naming her after a precious stone, maybe Ruby or Pearl

Luciana: What about a flower? Jasmine is a flower, right?

Shawna: Something exotic

Jasmine: A hothouse flower? Like Orchid?

Isabella: I love Orchid!

Aleecia: Better than Squirt!

///

Orchid—that was it! Orchid Watson. No, I couldn't use his last name on the birth certificate. Not without telling him and I wasn't about to do that. I don't even really know if he was the father. It could have been anyone at the party, I suppose, but I doubted it. Eddie had been groping me—I remembered that much. I would name her Orchid Walker. I sent friend requests to all the girls who had posted; I had found my posse.

//

One morning as I was opening up the store, Mr. Fong approached me. "You going to have baby?" he asked.

My swollen belly was stretching the shirt of my uniform, threatening to pop the buttons. I had been meaning to request a larger one.

"Yes, Mr. Fong," I said. "I'm pregnant."

"You have husband?" he asked.

"No," I said. "No husband."

"You need childcare?" he asked in his Asian accent. "My daughter run child care center."

"Let me guess—she lives in the neighborhood? How much does she charge?" I asked.

"I call her," he said. He pulled out his phone and dialed his daughter. They spoke in Chinese for a few minutes and then he shoved his phone at me. "She say she need to talk to you."

"Hello?" I said into the phone.

"Hi, this is Cindi." She spoke perfect English.

"I'm Jasmine," I said. "I work for your dad. My baby is due in September. Do you take infants?"

"We can take him at six weeks," she said.

"It's a girl," I said. "Orchid."

"We can take her at six weeks," she repeated.

"How much?" I asked.

"One twenty-five a week," Cindi said.

"Okay, good to know," I said. I could never afford that! I was starting to feel panicked. I couldn't possibly afford rent and food and childcare. How was this going to work?

"You need to reserve a spot," Cindi said. "It's two fifty to reserve a spot for November."

"I need to think about it," I said.

"Just give the check to my dad," Cindi said, and hung up.

Wow, I hadn't even thought about the cost of childcare. I was going to need to make more money. As soon as I could pop this baby out, I would have to get back into shape, fast, and get Bally's to hire me back.

Back at the register, I logged onto Facebook. My girls were still there, hanging out.

Jasmine: What do you plan to do about childcare?

No response.

Jasmine: Hello? Anybody there?

Candace: My little sister is my Lamaze coach. I guess she'll help out? My mom won't have anything to do with it. Maybe I can pay the housekeeper to watch Squirt?

Shawna: You have a housekeeper?

Jasmine: You guys haven't thought about this?

Aleecia: I need to finish high school and my mom works full-time.

This was depressing. I needed to log out.

//

"You're not gaining enough weight," Dr. Finch said at my monthly check-up in August. "Are you eating enough complex carbs? The baby needs carbs to grow."

"Her name is Orchid," I said.

"Pretty," she said. "Orchid needs carbs."

"I eat tons of fruits and vegetables," I said. "And whole grains," I added.

"That's a great start. Think about adding some other healthy carbs like beans and legumes. How about some whole grain bread and pasta?" she said. "Pasta with meat sauce. And garlic bread. Oh, now I'm making myself hungry."

Her laugh was contagious and we both doubled over.

When I had caught my breath I said, "Okay—spaghetti and meatballs tonight. How does that sound, Orchid?"

"And garlic bread," said Dr. Finch. "Am I invited?"

"Ooh!"

"What is it, Jasmine?" asked Dr. Finch.

"She kicked," I said.

"See, I'm telling you—she wants carbs!" Dr. Finch said, making me laugh again.

"What are you doing for exercise?" Dr. Finch asked.

"I swim every night after work," I said. "It's a small pool—mostly I just tread water."

"That's good," Dr. Finch said. "Don't overdo it."

"I can't wait to get back in shape," I said. "I'll need to lose thirty pounds to get my old job back."

"Breast-feed," Dr. Finch said. "You'll lose the baby weight—don't be in such a rush. I'm more worried that she'll be born underweight, and then you'll have real trouble on your hands. You'll be out of work much longer if she's not thriving. Take care of her now, and you'll both be much happier later."

Nine

MOM FLEW OUT THE THIRD WEEK OF SEPTEMBER. "You don't have a sofa?" she complained.

"You could stay in a motel," I suggested.

"It's cheaper to buy an airbed," she said. "Let's go to Wal-Mart."

At Wal-Mart, Mom grabbed a crib/playpen thingy and tossed in a year's supply of diapers and formula.

"I'm planning to breastfeed," I protested.

"You'll ruin your boobs," she said. "Look what happened to mine."

"Dr. Finch said I need to breast-feed to get my figure back," I said.

"Sure," she said. "Your waist, your hips. But what about your boobs? You'll never get your boobs back. We're talkin' curb-feelers. I can't remember the last time I saw my navel."

"Geez, Mom! Gross!" I said. "I'll get a boob job. Whatever! Besides you were twenty-six when you had me. I'm only nineteen."

"Oh now, she's gettin' bitchy," Mom said. "Here we go. I didn't fly all the way out here for the sassy backtalk."

"Sorry, Mom," I said. "Can we just get this stuff and go back to the apartment? I need to lie down."

"You and me both," she said.

//

Orchid was born on September 21st. It was a warm, sunny afternoon. Of course I don't remember that part of it. I remember the overly-lit maternity suite and pain, a lot of pain—and tons of screaming.

And then, there she was—my precious Orchid.

All healthy six pounds of her. All those carbs had paid off. My baby was a chubby little piece of chocolate. I wanted to gobble her up. Mom was in the bar down the street—seventeen hours of labor was too much for her. But I didn't care. I held my baby. Her eyes were open and her mouth was a pink oval. Nurse Ramone adjusted her to see if she would take the nipple. We tried several times but Orchid kept closing her eyes and drifting off to sleep. Nurse Ramone nudged her mouth to where it needed to be and she finally latched on.

"She's hungry!" Nurse Ramone exclaimed.

There's something about watching a newborn open her eyes and see her mom for the first time and knowing instinctively where to go for food. I pressed my lips to her head and sniffed her powdery scent. She wrinkled her little forehead and made little squeaking noises like a baby seal. *I am so in love!* I thought. *I am going to be a good mommy for you. I am going to be the best mommy! I just need to*

find a job and we need to find a sitter. We'll figure
this out. I could feel my blood pressure rising.

"Take our picture!" I handed Nurse Ramone
my phone.

///

I posted the photo on Facebook.

Isabella: Is that your baby?

Jasmine: Orchid was born at two this morning

Aleecia: So beautiful!

Candace, Shawna, and Luciana liked this post.

///

Mom had to get back to work, so she left two days
after the birth and I was left alone with Orchid.
I couldn't have been happier. Being a mom isn't
as hard as they say. It all seemed to come natu-
rally to me. When Orchid cried, I immediately

understood what she wanted: a diaper change, food, attention, whatever! I was cut out for motherhood.

"You're okay for money?" Mom called from the airport. "Not that I have any to spare."

"Thanks, Mom. I've saved up money from working at the car wash," I said. "I'm okay for a few months. Classes don't start again until January. I have time to figure everything out."

//

"If we're going to make this work, you're going to need to go to day care and I need to get a job." I had taken to talking to Orchid as though she were my life partner. She never argued with me, so I knew that we were in this together.

"So we're agreed?" I asked.

Orchid stared at me and sucked on her pacifier.

"Okay then," I said. "I need to find a ballet class that offers child care. Is there such a thing?"

The YMCA offered classes in ballet, Pilates, and Zumba. I signed up for everything and Orchid accompanied me every day.

"We don't usually take babies under six months of age," said Hannah, the child care manager at the Y.

"I make my living as a dancer," I said. "I need to get in shape fast so I can pay my rent."

"You'll have to sign a waiver," Hannah said.

"She'll be good," I said. "I promise. And if she cries, just wave at me. I'll leave class to come get her." *Yes!* I thought as I raced to the gym where the class was starting to warm up. *Finally, something is going my way.*

Orchid and I went to the Y every day and Hannah soon started wearing my Baby Björn to keep Orchid quiet while she tended to the older children. And it wasn't long before she started anticipating our arrival and rushed out to meet us as I was checking in at the front desk. Orchid greeted her with a big gummy smile and I was filled with jealousy but also gratitude as Hannah scooped her up and whisked her away.

///

Dr. Finch and Mom were both right. I was back down to one hundred and ten pounds within a month, but my boobs were engorged, laced with veins that I had never seen before. No topless dancing for me. But I started checking out Backstage.com every day, looking for auditions.

"Hannah," I said as I checked in one day. "Can you watch Orchid while I run across town for a casting call? I'll only be a few hours."

"You can't leave her here at the Y," Hannah said.

"Of course not," I said. *Damn,* I thought. *I've*

got to find someone to sit Orchid. "I meant are you available to babysit outside of the Y?"

"Sure," she said. "I guess it depends on when. I work nine to five."

Well, this won't work, I thought. *The auditions are usually at ten and two.*

"Never mind, then." I tried hard not to let the frustration register in my voice. "I'll have to figure something else out." *How am I supposed to do this?* I must have been a little rough as I yanked Orchid back from her.

"Hey, is everything okay?" Hannah said. She sounded alarmed.

"I'm fine," I lied. "Give me your number. I'll call you."

"Take my cell," Hannah said. "Let me know if you need me evenings or weekends."

//

That night, I called Cindi Fong.

"Hi Cindi, remember me?" I said into the phone. "I used to work for your dad?"

"I don't have any openings right now," Cindi said. "I never got your deposit."

"Can you take her part-time?" I asked. "Just a few hours once or twice a week while I go on auditions?" *Please, please, please,* I prayed.

"I'm licensed for ten kids," she said. "I'm full right now. If I get an opening I'll call you but you'd need to pay for a full-time slot even if she's only here for a few hours a week."

Fuck! I hung up.

Ten

"**O**RCHID, WHAT ARE WE GOING TO DO WITH YOU?" I asked. I paced anxiously back and forth across the living room. "What are we going to do, what are we going to do, what are we going to do?"

She gave me a big smile.

Just then, my neighbor, Mrs. Meacham, walked past on the balcony outside my window. I raced to the door. She was turning the key in her door, three apartments down from me.

"Mrs. Meacham, hi!" I shouted.

"How are you, Jasmine?" she asked. "How is baby Orchid?"

"She's doing great," I said. "Would you like to see her? Could we come by and visit?"

"That would be lovely, dear," she said. "Come help me with my groceries."

I slipped Orchid into her Baby Björn and walked over to Mrs. Meacham's apartment, trying to act nonchalant.

She was in the kitchen unloading her bags of groceries.

"Sit down," I said. "Let me do that."

Mrs. Meacham sighed and sank into her recliner.

"Can you hold Orchid?" I asked. I handed the baby to her.

While I unloaded the groceries and folded up the bags, I explained to Mrs. Meacham that I had been working out at the Y every day and was ready to get out there and start auditioning but I needed to find someone to watch Orchid.

"Do you think you could watch her for me?" I asked. "Just for a few hours?"

"Sure, honey," she said. "When were you thinking?"

"Right now?" I asked.

She started to protest but I interrupted her. "I know, I know, it's very short notice. But there is a casting call at two and if I leave now I can just make it. I should be back by five and I'll cook dinner for you."

"Well, alright," she said. "Can you feed her and change her before you leave? What will I do if she gets hungry?"

"I'll leave a couple of bottles of breast milk in your fridge," I said, thanking myself for the hundredth time for investing in that breast pump. "Thanks Mrs. Meacham, you're the best!"

I gave Orchid a big kiss and dashed to my car.

///

I needn't have rushed. There were more than fifty girls auditioning for a single opening. The director was calling the girls on to the stage, ten at a time. He walked them through a two-minute routine and then called out, "Next!" When it was my turn in the lineup, I locked eyes with him and tried to keep eye contact for the entire two minutes.

As I was leaving, the assistant director, Anne, called me over.

"I saw on your CV that you were in *Bacchanal*?" she asked.

"Yes," I said. "The late show."

"Ah," Anne said. "I thought I recognized you. Why did you leave?"

"I got pregnant," I said. "Just getting back to work now."

"Won't they take you back?" Anne asked.

"I can't dance that role, anymore," I said gesturing at my breasts, which had starting weeping through my leotard. "Speaking of which, I need to get back to my baby."

That was dumb, I thought as I walked out.

Maybe I had just talked myself out of a job? Nah, she wasn't planning to hire me anyway.

//

I made Mrs. Meacham a nice pork roast with mashed potatoes, green beans, and corn bread.

"Maybe you should look for a job as a cook?" she suggested.

"Maybe a personal chef?" I added, laughing. I tried to sound lighthearted but I was starting to panic. What if nobody would hire me? What if Eddie had blackballed me? Was I just wasting my time running to auditions?

The next day, I thought about what Anne had said and left a message for Geri. I said I was feeling much better and had started auditioning. I asked her to let me know if she had any openings. I figured I could address the costume issue later.

She never called me back. *Fuck!*

I texted Katrina: How r u?

Katrina: Hey kid, how are you? Where are you working?

Me: I'm just getting back to looking for work. Is Bacchanal hiring?

Katrina: Not that I know of—did you try Eddie?

Me: I left a message for Geri

Katrina: He fired Geri. The new guy is Kent

Fuck, fuck, fuck! I thought as I tried to sound breezy.

Me: Let's grab coffee next week?

Katrina: How about Tuesday?

Me: K

//

On Tuesday morning, I walked into Roxy's Diner with Orchid strapped into her Baby Björn.

"Oh my God!" Katrina said. "This is why you left the show?"

I shrugged and nodded. In the stark light of

day, Katrina looked a lot older. Her bleached hair was the texture of cotton candy forming a halo around her face. Maybe she wore a wig when she was working in the show?

"Let me hold her," Katrina said. "Come here, baby!"

Katrina tried to cradle Orchid, but she kept squirming. Then, Katrina gave her a spoon to play with and she settled down. The waitress came over.

"Do you want something to eat?" Katrina asked me. "The pumpkin pancakes here are great." To the waitress she said, "I'll have the fruit plate with yogurt and black coffee."

My stomach was growling but I only had three fives in my wallet and I needed to buy gas. "Just herbal tea and toast for me, thanks," I said.

"Do tell," Katrina said once the waitress was gone. "Where did this little one come from?"

"Remember Eddie's Christmas party?" I said.

"Yeah?" Katrina said.

"Good," I said. "I'm glad you do, because I don't remember a thing. I remember being in the pool with Eddie and the next morning I woke up in his bed. And then nine months later, this little one pops out. Surprise!" I didn't mean to sound sarcastic. I loved Orchid with my whole heart. "That didn't come out right."

"Don't be silly," Katrina said. "This is a big deal. It's not really my place to ask but did you consider having an abortion?"

"No," I said. "I wasn't raised that way."

"I get it," Katrina said.

"What happened that night?" I asked.

"Do you remember the guy with the Bentley?" Katrina asked.

"I remember the car," I said. "But I don't think I met the guy."

"You met him. He was passing out pills," Katrina said. "Oxy or something. You weren't the only one—a few girls passed out. The Bentley guy took a couple of the girls home with him."

"I took pills?" I asked.

"No, you refused," Katrina said. "I think you were actually trying to leave. You were getting out of the pool when Eddie took your glass. He must have slipped something into your drink."

Eleven

"ARE THE OTHER GIRLS OKAY?" I ASKED. "ANY OTHER little bundles of joy show up recently?"

Katrina laughed. "As far as I know, you're the only casualty. But look what Santa brought you!" She snuggled her face in Orchid's tummy. "I want one!"

"How did you stay sober?" I asked. "Where were you in all of this?"

"That's just it," Katrina said. "Eddie knows I'm eighteen months sober. I was sitting by the pool enjoying a ginger ale, watching the debacle unfold."

"How did I get upstairs?" I asked.

"You were out cold," Katrina said. "We didn't want you to drown. Eddie bundled you in a big towel and we carried you up."

"We?" I asked, incredulous. "We?"

"Look, you're a big girl," Katrina said. "How was I supposed to know that you weren't using birth control? And maybe you were his girlfriend. What do I know?"

"Girlfriend?"

"Eddie has been with every girl in the show," Katrina said. "Maybe you were his thing at the time. Whatever."

"You've slept with Eddie?" I asked. This conversation had become surreal.

"Oh, c'mon," Katrina said. "You knew that Eddie got around. He's the reason I joined AA. That's when I realized I had hit bottom."

"I'd heard rumors," I said. "I can't say that I *knew* that for a fact. Nobody warned me."

The waitress had delivered our order. I sipped my tea and contemplated this information.

"What should I do now?" I asked.

"Well, you could hit him with a paternity suit," Katrina said. "You and Orchid would be set for life. You gotta admit, she has Eddie's eyes."

Eddie had pale blue eyes—like a Siamese cat. Mine were hazel. Orchid definitely had his eyes.

"Or you could just come in for an audition," Katrina said. "See if he hires you back. I think you need to confront him."

"I can't dance topless anymore," I said. "My boobs are ruined."

"Just tell him that," Katrina said. "Not that you're ruined. Just that you don't do nude anymore. See what he says."

Could I trust Katrina's advice? She had helped Eddie carry me upstairs. If she were my friend, wouldn't she have insisted on driving me home? Why would she want me to audition for Eddie? Maybe she enjoyed watching the "debacle unfold." Maybe she wanted to watch Eddie squirm. Or maybe she wanted to watch him reject me.

"Katrina, I need to know," I said. "Did anyone else come upstairs with you—or after you? Is it possible that anybody else at the party could be Orchid's father?"

"You mean like a gang-rape, or something like that?" Katrina said. "No fucking way—Eddie isn't good at sharing."

"You know, I gotta go," I said. I dropped a five on the table and gathered up Orchid's things.

"Busy Mommy day?" Katrina asked.

Okay, this chick was definitely not my friend. But she had confirmed for me that Eddie was definitely the father.

"Dance class, auditions," I said. "You know the drill."

"Call Eddie." Those were her last words.

//

I was not going to call Eddie. Not if he were the last man on earth. What if he wasn't alone that night? What if he had invited other guys upstairs that night, and the paternity test came out negative? I wasn't going to let him humiliate me that way. I'm a smart girl, I reminded myself. I can dance and cook and I'm great at math. Orchid and I would figure this out on our own.

My bank balance was nearing zero, but I didn't want to call Mom. She would just insist that I come home, tail between my legs, admitting defeat. I wasn't ready for that. Every morning I got up and scoured Backstage.com, circling in red everything that I was remotely qualified for—dance teacher, paid extra. Most of the listings were for reality shows being shot in LA. I would barely qualify for *TeenMom—hmmm, what about pitching them an idea: knocked-up showgirl?* No! I would never submit Orchid to such humiliation.

At least once a week, I saw something that looked promising and I would dash down to Mrs. Meacham's apartment and beg her to watch Orchid for a few hours. She would resist but most days eventually capitulated to my promise of home cooking.

Today was not one of those days.

I saw the ad and thought, this is it!

Wynn Theater is casting for its water ballet spectacular, Dream Sequence! Seeking male and female singers and dancers to join the cast of the hottest ticket in Las Vegas!

I ran down the balcony and tapped on the door. "Mrs. Meacham are you home?" Tap, tap, tap. "Mrs. Meacham?" No answer. She had said something about visiting her daughter in Los Angeles. *Shit!*

I gotta do this, I'm gonna get this one. I was on the synchronized swim team in high school—we went to the nationals. *I am perfect for this! I can do this!*

I ran back to my apartment and grabbed a diaper, lotion, and a clean onesie.

"C'mon Orchid," I cooed. "Let's go baby. I know, I know," I said to her protestations. "Help Mommy now. Let's get you changed and ready."

Downstairs, I buckled Orchid into her car seat but she continued to whimper as we inched through traffic.

"What is it, baby? "I asked. "You never fuss like this."

My mind was racing. Should I carry her in with me and ask someone to watch her while I auditioned? What if she started crying?

"Don't blow this for me, Orchid," I said. "C'mon, settle down." I started humming "Rock-A-Bye Baby" to see if I could coax her to sleep.

Should I try to find someone on the hotel staff that would watch her for a couple of hours? I wondered if the Wynn offered a babysitting service for guests. What hadn't I researched this before I had left the house?

Finally we pulled into the parking garage of the Wynn. I wasn't sure of my plan until I found myself navigating to an empty spot in a remote corner of the desolate third level and parked as far away from as I could from any other cars. *This should be safe*, I thought.

"Here, baby, take your pacifier," I said. "That's a good girl. Mommy won't be long. I'll run in and kick ass and I'll be right back." I had checked the ambient temperature on the dash just before I turned the car off. *Sixty-nine degrees. We're in a parking garage—not in the sun. She'll be okay, right?* I laid a baby blanket over the car seat and covered her face. Any random busybody might look in and think that the car seat was empty.

I glanced nervously around as I opened the door and saw nobody in sight. I gingerly closed the driver's side door and stepped back. She was quiet—maybe she was nodding off at last. Then I clicked the lock button on the remote. The car let out a loud beep, and she started to wail. I backed away from the car, hoping she would quiet down.

I turned and ran toward the elevator. But I could still hear her crying.

"What am I doing?" I said aloud. "I can't do this."

I ran back to the car and unlocked the door. It felt really warm inside the car. *Shit, I could have killed my baby. No job was worth that.*

"I'm so sorry, Orchid!" I unbuckled her from her car seat and opened my blouse to give her the nipple. She stopped crying and suckled loudly.

I wept as I rocked her in my arms. *Oh my baby,* I thought. *How could I have left you? What kind of a monster am I?*

"I think we need to go talk to your Daddy," I said. I sat in the car and nursed Orchid until she was sated and had fallen asleep.

Twelve

I WASN'T SURE HOW I WAS GOING TO GET TO EDDIE. IF I couldn't get through backstage security at Bally's I might have to go to his house.

I parked at Bally's and approached security. I was relieved to recognize the guard on duty.

"José, how are you?" I smiled and waved.

"Miss Jasmine, we haven't seen you in a while," he said.

"Well, yes, I've been a little busy having a baby." I turned sideways so he could see her face.

"What a beauty," he said. "Just like her Mommy."

"I have a meeting with Eddie," I lied. "Is he in his office?"

José checked the log. "Yes," he said. "He should be. He hasn't left the building."

"Thanks!" I said. "I don't have my ID. Can you log me in as a visitor?"

"Just need your photo ID," José said. "And hers."

I must have registered a look of panic.

"I'm kidding!" he said, laughing. "It's good to see you. Are you coming back to work?"

"I hope so," I said. I handed him my driver's license. "That's what I'm here to speak with Eddie about."

"Well, you have a nice day," José said, handing me back my license.

//

My heart was in my throat as I entered the hallway to Eddie's office. I stood outside his door practicing what I was going to say.

Hey, would you like to meet your daughter? Or

how about, *What exactly happened the night of your Christmas party?*

Just then the door swung open and a man walked out. Early forties, wiry, well-dressed, I figured this must be Kent. He nearly plowed into us.

"Oh, I'm sorry," Kent said. "I didn't see you there. Do you have a meeting with Eddie?"

"Hi, I'm Jasmine," I said. "I was in the show last winter. I wanted to pop in and say hi to Eddie."

"Sure," he said. He poked his head inside Eddie's office. "Eddie, Jasmine is here to see you."

Oh shit, I thought. *Here we go.*

"Thanks," I smiled at Kent as I walked through the doorway.

"Close the door, please," Eddie said to Kent. Kent shut the door and I stood there facing Eddie with Orchid strapped to my chest like a fortification for my heart.

"Jazz, I'm surprised to see you," Eddie said. "Have a seat."

I sat down on the couch and adjusted Orchid in her Baby Björn.

"How can I help you?" Eddie asked.

What do I do now? I thought. *Ask for a job or ask for child support? Both?*

"Here's the thing," I said. "The last time I saw you, I had just woken up naked in your bed."

His expression was blank. What was wrong with this guy? Was he going to pretend the party never happened?

"The Christmas party?" I asked. "Remember?"

"Mm-hm," he said.

"Then Geri fired me in February, and right after that, I found out I was pregnant," I said.

"Congratulations," he said.

Obviously I needed to spell this out for him. "Eddie, I'm pretty sure she's yours," I said. "I haven't been with anyone in three years and I'm assuming we had sex that night?" *I don't have the courage to use the word "rape,"* I thought. *I need his help.* "Although I don't remember anything after I got into the pool with you."

"Well, if you don't remember anything, why do you assume we had sex?" he asked.

Was he kidding? Did he need a lesson in the birds and the bees?

"Let's review," I said. My voice took on an edge. "I woke up naked in your bed in December, I gave birth in September. I believe we had sex."

"How do you know she's mine?" he asked.

"Well, she has your eyes," I said. "Which would be obvious to you except that she's asleep and I'm not going to wake her up. Or we could just get a paternity test."

Eddie's eyes narrowed. He took a long time to respond. "Sure, we can do that," he said. "And if she is mine, I will file for full custody and I will win. You got pregnant while working as a topless dancer. You probably don't have two nickels to rub together. What kind of home could you provide for her?"

I hoped he couldn't read the panic on my face. I had nearly abandoned my baby in a parking garage. Maybe it was even captured on the security camera. I would have gone to jail and they would have taken her away from me. He was right—what judge would rule that I was a fit parent? Man, this guy was good—of all the possible scenarios I had considered, I never figured he would threaten to take her away from me. I took a deep breath and decided to play the sympathy card.

"Eddie, you're right," I said. "I need to get back to work so I can provide for her. Can you get me a job in the show?"

"And we drop the paternity question?" he asked.

"Yes," I said. I felt ashamed.

"Talk to Kent," Eddie said. "Maybe he's looking for a temporary replacement. I'm not casting any new positions right now. Kent will know what's available. Good to see you, dear. Best of luck."

///

I knew there was no point in talking to Kent. Eddie would never let him hire me back. The story might even get back to Katrina and the others that I had threatened Eddie with a paternity suit and he had countered with the threat of a custody suit. Shit, my name was surely going to be mud in this town.

I was fighting back tears as I passed through security and waved to José.

"Did you get to see Eddie?" José asked.

"Yes, thanks," I said.

"Take care," he said.

I will take care, I thought. *I will take care of you, Orchid. I will be the best mother that I know how to be. But how will I take care of you?*

//

When I got home I tucked Orchid into her crib and logged onto Facebook.

My girls were all there.

Aleecia: Kyle's mom's boyfriend threw him out of the house. Can you believe that?

Luci: I believe it. My mom threw me out!

Jasmine: Has anyone considered giving your baby up for adoption?

Candace: My mom made me interview with an adoption agency

Jasmine: And?

Candace: The baby-daddy has to agree to the adoption. It's complicated

Jasmine: And what if the baby-daddy doesn't want anything to do with the baby?

Isabella: Maybe not so complicated, right?

I logged off of Facebook and Googled adoption agencies. I discovered a website called Adoption-Services.org and filled out the "contact us" form. And then I waited.

Thirteen

THE NEXT MORNING THERE WAS A TEXT MESSAGE ON MY phone from a Dr. Victor Bergen: Call 800-943-0400 to schedule a confidential intake session. We will be happy to help you find a shelter, find financial, medical, and nutritional assistance programs, help you to find the perfect loving home for your child, or help you in some other way. Our primary concern is to make sure you and your baby are safe and healthy.

I steeped a pot of herbal tea and re-read the text message several times. Then Orchid woke up and I changed, nursed, and bathed her before returning to my phone to read the message yet again. She was lying in her playpen, gumming her stuffed bunny, when I placed the call.

"Hello, how can we help you?" the voice said.

"My name is Jasmine Walker," I said. "I got a text from you."

"Hello, Jasmine. My name is Caroline," the voice said. "Would you like to schedule an appointment to discuss our services?"

"Yes," I said.

"Are you available to come in today?" Caroline asked. "Around two?"

"Yes," I said.

I jotted down the address and put my phone down. I sat there for a long time watching Orchid gurgling and smiling, content with her toys and basking in the benevolent sun streaming through the window. The website said they offered financial assistance. All I really needed was someone to look after Orchid while I auditioned. I was glad I had placed the call.

After Orchid had her nap, I bundled her into

her car seat and headed across town to the address Caroline had given me. The office was on the second floor of a tan brick building behind a Methodist church. I parked in the visitor's lot and buckled Orchid into her Baby Björn.

"Let's go, baby," I said.

Upstairs, I checked in with the receptionist.

"I have an appointment with Caroline," I said.

"I'm Caroline," the receptionist said. She stood to greet me. "You must be Jasmine. And who is this little one?"

"Orchid," I said.

"How old?" Caroline asked.

"Two months," I said.

"Perfect," Caroline said. "Let me show you to the consultation room. Dr. Bergen will be with you shortly."

Perfect, I thought. *What did she mean by that?*

The room was furnished with a round table and four chairs. In the middle of the table, there was a speaker phone, a box of Kleenex, and an electronic console. There was a large flat-screen TV on one wall and the other walls were decorated with paintings of children at play. I paced around the room, nervously.

The door opened and a man walked in. He was tall and thin with wireframe glasses and thinning reddish hair.

"Hello, Jasmine," he said. "I'm Dr. Bergen. Thank you for coming in today. Would you like to sit down?"

"I think I'd rather stand," I said. "Orchid gets restless if I stop moving."

"Jasmine and Orchid," he said. "Exotic flowers, both of you."

That word, exotic, again. I was starting to feel jumpy. Maybe coming here was a bad idea.

"I'll sit, if you don't mind," he said. He opened a notebook and cocked his pen.

"What brings you in today?" Dr. Bergen asked.

"I need help with Orchid," I said. "I'm a dancer, or at least I was until I got pregnant. And

I can't afford childcare right now. But I need to find someone to watch her while I'm going on auditions."

"What do you know about the birth father?" Dr. Bergen asked.

"I'm not sure what you're asking?" I said.

"Are you in touch with the birth father?" he asked.

"No," I said. "I'm not certain who the birth father is." That was not actually a lie.

"Do you have family in the area?" he asked. "Any kind of a support system?"

"No," I said. "My mom is in New Jersey and I wouldn't exactly call her supportive." I paused. "That's not totally fair—she sends me money when she can."

"Have you considered adoption, Jasmine?" Dr. Bergen took off his glasses and set them on the notepad. "There are dozens of loving couples in the Las Vegas area who can't have children of their own."

"Your website mentioned financial assistance," Jasmine said. "I want to keep my baby."

"Yes," Dr. Bergen said. "Our office can help you sign up for AFDC, Medicaid, and food stamps if that is what you would like. We also can refer you to a homeless shelter for women with children."

Homeless shelter, welfare, food stamps? The words stung like knives in my throat. I pulled out a chair and sat down.

"What are my other options?" I asked.

"Would you like to browse our database of adopting families?" Dr. Bergen pushed a couple of buttons on the console and the lights dimmed and the TV went on. Up came an image of an interracial couple holding hands. Dr. Bergen swung the console around to face me. "You can click here to play an audio file for each couple. And then click the arrow here to advance to the next profile."

"I don't want to give up my baby," I said.

"Have you ever felt overwhelmed with the responsibility of having a child?" he asked. "You're young, you haven't finished college, right?"

"Right," I said.

"Have you ever been tempted to leave your child home alone while you went to work, or leave her in a locked car?"

I panicked. *How did he know about that?*

"You read about it in the paper all the time, the harried, overwhelmed parent forgetting about the baby in the back seat or that poor woman in Arizona who left her baby in the car while she went inside for a job interview. So sad," he said.

Silence hung between us for a long moment.

"How does this work?" I asked. "This adoption thing?"

Dr. Bergen leaned forward. He seemed a little too eager. "You have choices—open or closed adoption," he said. "Closed adoption means that you prefer to remain anonymous to the adopting family and you agree to have no future contact with them or your child."

"Will she ever know who I am?" I asked.

"Not without your explicit consent," Dr. Bergen said.

"And what about the other kind—open adoption?" I asked.

"It's kind of like a dating site. You choose whom you'd like to meet and you can meet as many couples as you like," he said. "We will facilitate the meetings and guide you through the interview process. There is no time pressure. You take as long as you need to find the right fit. Once we've found a match, you and the adopting family can choose to have regular communications—updates on your child's well-being, that sort of thing. The adopting family may also agree to occasional visits. Or you may choose to have no contact until the child is eighteen."

I rested my cheek against Orchid's head and inhaled her baby scent. I started to cry.

I looked up at Dr. Bergen. "The most important thing is that Orchid must know how much I loved her," I said. "She can never think that I gave her up because I didn't love her."

Fourteen

DR. BERGEN NUDGED THE BOX OF KLEENEX TOWARD ME. I took a handful.

"We can draft that language into the contract," Dr. Bergen said. "Some birth mothers write a letter with instructions that it be given to the child when she starts to ask questions about her origins."

"How would you like to proceed?" Dr. Bergen asked. "Would you like to be left alone to browse our gallery? As you scroll through the profiles, you can tap the plus sign on the console to add them to your favorites and the minus button will remove them from your personal gallery. Once you've selected your top choice, we'll contact the family to schedule a meeting. Sound good?"

Dr. Bergen stood up to leave. "Can I get you some water or coffee?"

"Water would be good," I said. "Thanks."

"Just press the call button on the console when you're done and Caroline will buzz me," he said. "Jasmine, you are doing a very loving thing."

Loving thing, loving thing, I repeated to myself as I rocked Orchid in her carrier. *It's the right thing, baby. I thought I could take care of you but I can't. I don't have a job, I don't have any money. You need a mommy who can give you everything you need. Even if I take you home to New Jersey, we're still in the same situation. I just can't see my way out of it.*

I rang the call button.

I chose Allison Martin. Her husband, Griffin, seemed nice enough but Allison's story spoke to me. She was forty-two and had miscarried twice before her first husband, Jackson, died in

Afghanistan. Apparently Griffin had a low sperm count, so Allison's only option was adoption. Allison was of mixed race and Jackson had been African-American. Griffin looked Irish to me.

Allison was tall and slender; Griffin was an inch or so shorter than her. He was very muscular but had a bit of a potbelly. He was a retired autoworker and had moved to Las Vegas to care for his elderly mother. Allison was a nurse at the assisted living facility, where Griffin's mother had lived until her death the previous year.

///

I held Orchid tight as I counted the days to the first meeting. Too tight. She would squirm and fuss but I couldn't put her down. I was terrified if I put her down, she would never let me pick her up again. At night, I dreamed that she had disappeared; I had lost her somewhere. Did I leave her at the Y? Had she fallen in the pool? *Where are you Orchid?* I screamed in my dream but no sound came out of my mouth.

//

The first time, we met in Dr. Bergen's office. I left Orchid in the nursery next door. Dr. Bergen led us through a series of exercises, designed to uncover our inherent beliefs about parenthood and child rearing. Griffin had two adult children living in Ohio who he visited every few months. He seemed very close to them, and I liked that. Allison was originally from Oklahoma and was part Shawnee. She had a large extended family spread out across Nevada, Arizona and Oklahoma. Orchid would have a lot of cousins—that was something I had always wanted for her. I was an only child, and Mom wasn't close to her brothers. I never really knew my cousins.

For our second meeting, I suggested that Allison and I have lunch together. Dr. Bergen warned us that it was against protocol to exclude Griffin but I needed to speak with Allison alone if I was going to tell her the whole truth about Orchid.

"Can I hold her?" Allison asked as soon as we got seated.

Orchid was awake and staring at the people around us. I stood and handed her to Allison.

"I didn't always work with old folks, you know," Allison said. "I used to work in maternity. I have a lot of experience with babies."

"Why did you make the switch?" I asked.

"More jobs in geriatrics these days," Allison said.

When our food arrived, I placed Orchid in her carrier and gave her a pacifier. "I'm still breast-feeding," I said. "I guess she'll need to transition to formula." Then I looked up at Allison and said, "I need to tell you about Orchid's conception. You will let her keep her name, Orchid, I hope?"

"Griff and I already discussed it," Allison said. "We love the name Orchid."

I let out a huge sigh. "I really have no right to

ask, but I am so happy to hear that." I took a long drink of water and then set my glass down before continuing. "Look, you can decide how much of this you want to share with Orchid when the time is right."

I told Allison the story of the Christmas party, waking up in Eddie's bed and finding myself pregnant two months later.

"I wanted you to know that I'm not some slut who slept around and had no idea who father was," I said. "But when I confronted Eddie, he threatened to file for custody, and I couldn't risk losing her to him. So there is no proof of paternity. Which is better, all things considered. He probably would try to muck up the adoption process. The most important thing is that Orchid needs to know how much I wanted her and how much I loved her, do love her. I tried to keep her and make it on my own."

Allison recoiled in horror. "Do you think he'll come after us and sue for custody?"

"Not a chance in hell," I said. "He only said

that to scare the shit out of me, which it did. I don't have any money. I can't fight him in court. He knows that. He just wanted me to disappear. He wanted Orchid to disappear. This solves all of his problems." I felt nauseous but I knew I was right.

Allison reached across the table and held my hand in both of hers. Her eyes were wet.

"And one more thing, as long as I'm asking," I said.

"What is it?" Allison asked.

"Promise me you'll pay for dance lessons if she asks?" I said.

Allison laughed through her tears. "My mother was a dancer with the Oklahoma City Ballet."

"You're kidding!"

//

That clinched it. My final meeting with the Martins was in Dr. Bergen's office with attorneys present.

"Would you like to hold her?" Dr. Bergen said to me.

I was torn. I was giving up my baby. Would holding her make us feel better or far worse?

I nodded, silently. My heart was breaking. I got to hold my baby one last time and then I kissed her goodbye. Orchid Walker Martin was her new name.

Fifteen

MY APARTMENT SEEMED DESOLATE NOW THAT ORCHID was gone and I couldn't wait to get out of there and as far away from Las Vegas as possible. I started packing the next day.

I didn't own much. I donated all of Orchid's baby things to the Methodist church next door to the adoption agency. I emptied the kitchen cupboards and packed the non-perishables into boxes that I delivered to the food bank. I taped a sign to my front door, "Free Stuff," and the neighbors came over to pick through piles of books, glasses and dishware. I had to leave my futon on the sidewalk, but other than that, everything fit into my car. I found Orchid's stuffed bunny under the front seat of the car. I held it up to my face and inhaled. *Oh, Orchid!*

I knocked on the super's door.

"Goodbye, Mr. Fong," I said as I handed him my key.

"Will you be back in September?" he asked.

"No," I said. "Not this year. Maybe next year."

"Okay, next year," he said nodding. "See you."

Who am I kidding? I thought as I walked down the sundrenched walkway to the parking lot. *I'll never be back. I had my chance as a dancer. I screwed up, and now my life is changed forever.*

The drive to New Jersey took me five days. It was only technically thirty-eight hours of driving time but I had to stop every couple of hours to cry and I couldn't stay awake past dusk. The days got shorter and the roads icier as I made my way east. My breasts were engorged with breast milk that Orchid would never taste again, but WebMD said the agony should only last a few days.

I picked up a brochure at a Motel 6 outside of Omaha and plotted my trajectory according to the location of the Motel 6 closest to the five-hundred-mile mark. I hopscotched across the country, racing the eighteen-wheelers through Omaha, Denver, Davenport and Chicago to Cleveland and Allentown, where the signs started directing me toward New York City. Each night I would pull into the parking lot of the Motel 6, clutching my order from KFC or Pizza Hut. I would curl up in bed and fall asleep with the TV on. At night, I dreamed of driving—the rhythm of the tires on the freeway—*k-thump, k-thump*, mile after endless mile. In the middle of the night I would wake up with a start, wondering where I was, and where was Orchid. Then I would remember and collapse on the pillow with a heavy heart. The giddiness I had felt as I drove west three years before had been replaced by a sense of dread, of loss, of impending death. Once I had been racing toward something. Now, I was in retreat.

After what seemed like an eternity, I reached

Pennsylvania, but highway I-80 was under yet another phase of construction. Traffic slowed to a crawl for two hours. I hadn't been able to stretch at the ballet barre in days and my ass was killing me. With the skyline of Manhattan in the distance, at last I saw the sign for Route 46 to North Bergen.

I had texted Mom from the New Jersey border and she was waiting for me. It was always Christmas in my neighborhood of single-family homes clad in aluminum siding and wrought iron railings; the holiday decorations hung all year long. Mom jumped up from the couch as I pulled into the driveway and met me at the door.

"Where is that baby?" Mom cried out. "Where is my grandbaby? How can you drive for five days with a baby in the car? That poor baby, she needs to get some rest, now."

I stood on the porch with just a suitcase in my hand.

"What did you do with my grandbaby?" Mom demanded.

"Can I come in?" I asked.

"Sure," she said. "Sit your ass down and tell me what is going on."

"Hi, Mom," I said. "Nice to see you, too."

"Don't give me any of that lip," she said.

"Can I use the bathroom?" I asked.

I ran the washcloth under the faucet until it was steaming hot. Then I pressed it against my face, my chest and the back of my neck. I looked like hell. *This is the face of loss,* I thought as I gazed in the mirror. *Will this face ever recover? Will I ever be happy again?* I dried my face and steeled myself to face Mom.

She was sitting on the sofa, nursing a beer. I went into the kitchen to get myself one too.

"What have you gone and done?" she yelled out.

I walked slowly into the room, trying to lengthen and soften my spine after five days on the road.

I set my beer down on the table and did a couple of side-bends.

"Mom," I said at last. "I gave her up."

"What do you mean, you gave her up?" she demanded.

"I gave her up for adoption," I said. "I found a wonderful mother for Orchid—her name is Allison Martin. She is part black, part Indian, part something else, I guess. Her mom used to dance with the Oklahoma City Ballet. How great is that?"

Mom was quiet for a long time

"Is she married?" Mom asked at last.

"Yes," I said. "Her first husband died in Iraq or someplace. She's remarried. He has adult children from his first marriage, but they couldn't have kids of their own—Allison, I mean."

"Well, you've finally done the responsible thing," Mom said. "I never wanted you to move out there and Lord knows you have no business raising a baby. You found a good family to raise her. Amen. So what's your plan now? Are you dropping out of school? Because you're not going to just park your ass on my couch."

"I can transfer to Kean or Montclair," I said. "I

think I have a couple of weeks before the deadline for fall admission."

"You're not going back to Vegas?" she asked.

"You were right about that place, Mom," I said, flopping into a chair. "You were right about a lot of things." I took a long draw from my beer. "I miss her so much! Allison said she would post photos on Facebook every day so I can watch Orchid grow up."

"Do you think that is wise?" Mom asked. "In my day, you kissed your illegitimate baby good-bye and went on with your life. You're twenty years old. You have your whole life ahead of you. And Orchid is in a better place, now. She's better off without you."

Okay, that stings, I thought. "Oh my God, you make it sound like she's dead!" I said. "I wonder if she's missing me."

"You said you found Orchid a good mother," Mom said. "If you pine over her every day, you'll never move on with your life".

Mom dimmed the table lamp and we sat in the half-darkness for a long time.

"Did you ever consider giving me up for adoption?" I asked.

"Not for one minute," she said. "Twenty years ago, things were different. You would have most likely ended up in a foster home. Of course things were hard in the beginning. After your daddy ran off with that fool, Irene, my momma wouldn't have nothing to do with me. I had to move us back in with my grandma."

"Do you think I've made a mistake?" I asked.

"You've made your bed—now lie in it," she said.

"Speaking of making beds," I said. "I need to stay here for a while. Just until I get a job."

"You show up here, unannounced," she said. "Texting me like I'm some teenager? And now you say you're staying for a while? Is this the way I raised you? You moved to Las Vegas against my wishes. Then you refused to come back when I told you to. You gave up my grandchild without consulting me. What am I, your doormat?"

"I'm sorry, Mom," I said. "I need a do-over. I need a fresh start. I always thought I could come home if I didn't know where else to go."

"Well, I wasn't planning on that," she said. "But you can clean out the spare room and make up the bed in there. There is still a lot of Christmas stuff that needs to be put away. Maybe you can do that tomorrow?"

"Sure," I said.

I dragged my roller bag upstairs to the spare room and shoved the wrapping paper, ribbon and boxes of ornaments that were burying the bed onto the floor. I made up the bed with clean sheets, shut the light and curled up in bed with Orchid's stuffed bunny.

Sixteen

TWO DAYS LATER, MOM DISCOVERED A LEAK IN THE
upstairs shower. She called her insurance
adjuster and he declared that the pipes had to be
replaced. That would mean ripping out the tile
and everything.

"Basically, you'll get a whole new bathroom for
the cost of your deductible," the adjuster said.

"Well aren't we glad that you're home, now?"
Mom said to me.

"This is my project?" I protested. "Mom, I need
to find a job."

"In between job-hunting, you can deal with contractors and shit," she said. "I have a route to drive."

For the next three weeks, I fielded texts from contractors and potential employers and dashed back and forth between interviews, classes at Mom's Y, and deliveries. Every now and then, I'd pause at the door of the childcare room at the Y and inhale the scent of freshly diapered babies.

True to her word, Allison posted photos of Orchid every day. She was no longer getting breast milk and was putting on weight.

Geez, I hope she doesn't turn out to be a fat kid, I thought.

There were pictures of Allison holding Orchid, obviously drunk with maternal delight.

That should be me, I thought. Then I caught myself. Maybe Mom was right about this too. Maybe I should un-friend Allison. I wasn't sure I wanted to see her looking so happy with my baby. Adoption in the days before Facebook must have been so much easier.

Every day I checked Backstage.com and then I finally hit pay dirt. Elaine's in Cape May was hiring dancers for a dinner theater show. It was a two-and-a-half-hour drive each way without traffic, but it was work, the tips were supposed to be good, and I would be dancing professionally again. And it's not like I had to rush home to feed a baby or anything.

I drove down for the audition on a Tuesday. The manager was a greasy guy named Guido.

"Ladies!" he shouted. "We need to see cleavage. This is a big selling point. Nothing less than a C-cup. Please!"

I flashed back to the audition for *Bacchanal*. Please God, don't make us strip down for this.

A handful of girls packed up their gym bags and left.

"Okay, the rest of you," Guido shouted. "Tap-dancing! Show us your stuff."

Tap-dancing and cleavage, I thought. What

kind of a show was this? Hey, it was Cape May, I reminded myself.

Guido put us through our paces, tap, burlesque, and a few moves that I was familiar with from my time in Vegas.

"Okay," Guido shouted. "Let's see how you look in costume."

We were herded into the locker room and handed what looked like beer-hall-wench costumes. Low-cut, off-the-shoulder peasant blouse, with a strap-up bustier and a short, flared skirt. Fishnet stockings completed the look.

We suited up and pranced back out onstage to pose wench-like. It was silly and actually sort of fun. We were play-acting at looking sexy in a PG sort of way. This was a family-friendly show, after all. I was struck by the sharp contrast with the raw sexuality and cutthroat environment of Vegas.

I got the gig.

//

We had three weeks of rehearsals before opening night. Since we were the actual waitresses as well as the performers, we had to learn the menu and also practice carrying heavy trays of food while wearing spiked heels. We also had to practice the famous dip as perfected by the original Playboy bunnies. When serving food or drink, heels together and bend from the waist.

Once the show opened, I only had to work on weekends—dinner shows on Friday and Saturday and brunch on Sunday. Claudia, one of the other waitresses, had rented a cottage on the beach and invited a few of us to crash there. The place felt like a sorority house and I was grateful for the company.

The other girls tended to head home on Sunday nights, as they had other part-time jobs in Philly or New York. I had nothing to go home to, so unless Mom needed something done around the house, I stayed at Claudia's and we became close.

Cape May in the winter was really quite nice. It

was quiet; a lot of places were closed until April. The ocean was restless and made the beach a more interesting destination than in the summer months. Claudia and I went for long runs on the beach. She had been a gymnast in college and was working toward her certification as a Pilates instructor.

"Let's stop for a minute," Claudia said.

We slowed to a walk but the wind coming off of the ocean was biting, and within minutes the perspiration on my back started to freeze.

"Let's grab some coffee," I suggested. We turned inland and walked toward the boardwalk.

We ordered our drinks and found a table in a corner, far from the door.

"This was a great idea," I said. "Renting the cottage. I would never have thought of it. I would have spent all my time commuting to north Jersey."

"It's wonderful out here, isn't it?" Claudia asked. "My grandparents had a place out here and we spent all of our summers on the shore." She sipped her hot chocolate. After a few minutes, she lowered her voice and said, "I've had a rough year. I needed to get away from my real life for a bit."

"What's your real life?" I asked.

"I got pregnant by accident," she said. "My boyfriend accused me of plotting a conspiracy against him, to force him to marry me. Seriously? Who does that? And how could he think so little of me?"

"What happened?" I asked.

"He made me get an abortion," she said.

"He couldn't force you to get an abortion," I said.

"No," she responded. "But basically he said he wasn't going to marry me until I got an abortion."

"What?" I said. "That doesn't make any sense."

"It's not like I would marry him, after that," Claudia said. "But I'm twenty-one. I wasn't prepared to be a single mother."

"What happened to the boyfriend?" I asked.

"He wanted us to go on as though nothing had happened," she said. "What a joke! Can you believe he didn't even go with me to the clinic? He was in Colorado skiing with his rich friends. I had to beg my friend, Patty, to go with me. It was horrible. And then when I got home, this huge bouquet of flowers arrived. I threw the flowers away. It just made me sad to look at them. As if that's solace for the loss I was going through. Then he had the balls to call me from Colorado to tell me how sorry he was. He said all of his friends were dissing him for abandoning me to go on the stupid ski trip. And now he thinks we can just go on like before? What the fuck?"

I took a deep breath and absorbed what Claudia had just shared with me.

"I'm glad you feel you can talk to me about this," I said. "Here's my story. I'm not sure if it's better or worse. I had a baby in September. Eddie Watson, the choreographer of my show at Bally's, slipped something into my drink at a party and date-raped me. It wasn't really date rape, since we weren't on a date. I was at a party at his house and

I woke up the next morning in his bed. That's just rape. Anyway, I had the baby; her name is Orchid. Do want to see a picture?"

I dug my phone out of my purse and scrolled through my Photo Stream. I showed Claudia the one that Nurse Ramone took at Orchid's birth and then some of the pictures that Allison had posted to Facebook.

"Isn't she beautiful?" I asked.

"Oh my God!" Claudia said. "Where is she?"

Seventeen

I SET MY PHONE DOWN ON THE TABLE AND LOOKED AT Claudia. "I gave her up," I said. "I didn't mean to. I really tried to take care of her, but I couldn't find work and I couldn't afford childcare. I found a family; Allison lost her first husband in the war and her second husband was older. Allison is a great mom; I know she is taking amazing care of my baby. We're friends on Facebook, and she posts photos every day."

"Wow," Claudia said. "Which do you think is harder—losing your baby to abortion or adoption?"

"Either way, you think about them all the time, right?" I asked. "Wonder about the baby you didn't have or dream about the one you did and wonder where she is and what's she's doing."

"I think about it every day," Claudia said. Her eyes grew moist. "I'll never be an activist—pro-life or pro-choice."

"Yeah, me neither," I said. "I think those people haven't gone through what we have. It's a terrible predicament, and I don't believe it's anybody else's business what a woman chooses to do."

We finished our drinks and hit the ladies' room. Claudia took my hand in hers as we walked back to the cottage.

"Do you think you'll ever see Orchid again?" asked Claudia.

"I ask myself that question every day," I replied. "The Martins said they are open to me visiting anytime I want. I'm not sure I'm ready, though. I need to be in a better place psychologically— not working as a dancing waitress in some dorky dinner theater."

"Hey now!" Claudia said, laughing. "No, you're

right. I feel the same way. I'm saving up to open my own Pilates studio."

"I wish I had a dream like that," I said. "I have no idea what I want to do anymore."

///

The show had been running for several months, and as the weather warmed up, the crowds got bigger. Guido started talking about adding a show on Thursdays as well. The audience was mostly families, sometimes a bachelorette party or two, but every night there was at least one table of drunks—sometimes college kids, sometimes older guys. Guido always seemed to seat those tables in my section. It was a mixed blessing. Their bar tabs were big, and they tipped generously as long as I let them look down my blouse and put up with a little bit of groping which involved a hand on my waist or hip, sometimes my thigh or shoulder and inevitably being pulled onto someone's lap for the group photo.

But I didn't complain. They say that time heals all wounds and I was glad to be busy and found myself thinking about Orchid only once or twice a day instead of every waking minute. I mailed Allison a postcard every week in the hopes that she would save them for Orchid for when she was older.

//

I think it was an evening in early May when a group of high school girls came in, chaperoned by a couple of adults—teachers, probably.

"Guido, can I have that table?" I asked.

"Why? They probably won't tip," he said. But he grudgingly made some adjustments with his wax pencil on the table chart.

"Ladies, how are we doing tonight?" I said as they got seated. "Can I get anybody a beverage?"

The woman seated at the end of the table ordered soft drinks for the girls and a bottle of wine.

I recognized her voice.

"Ms. Gregory?" I asked.

She looked up and did a double take. "Jasmine?"

Ms. Gregory was my dance teacher all through high school. She had also coached my synchronized swim team.

"Is this the swim team?" I asked.

"Actually, I've opened a dance studio in Jersey City, and this is my inaugural class," she said. "Girls, I'd like to introduce Jasmine Walker, one of my star students. Last I heard you were dancing in a show in Las Vegas?"

"Yes, that's true," I said. "But I had some health issues so I came home to recuperate. Look, let me get your drinks and then I need to check on these other two tables, but I'll be back to take your order and we can chat later."

//

Her star student? How humiliating. What kind of

a role model did I look like to those girls? You can have all the talent in the world and look where you end up—dancing topless in Las Vegas or in a lame-ass dinner theater on the Jersey shore. I vowed at that moment to get my life and my career on track. I needed to stop letting life happen to me and take charge—go after what I wanted. I had gotten lazy, hanging out at the shore all weekend and had missed the application deadlines for school. I was depressed; I was in mourning. But that was no excuse.

"I'm sorry about the show," I said to Ms. Gregory as I handed her the check. "It's pretty lame."

"Nonsense, the girls loved it," she said. "You all looked like you were having fun and it was very entertaining."

She signed the credit card receipt and handed it back to me.

"I'd love to connect with you next week," she said. "Can we meet for coffee?"

"Sure," I said. "That would be great."

"There's a new coffee house that just opened

on Bay Street," she said. "I'll text you the address. Tuesday morning good for you?"

//

I got to the Warehouse Café early on Tuesday and ordered a medium dark roast, black, and found a seat by the window. I saw Ms. Gregory before she saw me. There was something about her that was different—the way she was dressed. She'd always been stylishly cool, but now she looked more professional and polished.

I waited until she'd gotten her coffee and then waved her over.

"You look great," I said.

"I'd been thinking a lot about you, Jasmine," she said. "I had no idea you were back in town."

"Well I wasn't really planning on it," I said. "But here I am. I'm only working as a waitress until I finish school." As soon as I said that, I regretted it. I hoped she didn't ask me about it. I wasn't even enrolled. Shit, I hadn't even applied. And after school, then what—work as a bookkeeper?

"That's what I wanted to talk to you about," Ms. Gregory said. "I've opened up my own dance school—oh right, I told you about that. Well, I've been looking for a partner and I kept thinking of you and wondered what you were up to. Someone told me that you were working in Vegas, and that didn't surprise me. When I called you my star student last week, I meant it. The things that really made you stand out when you were studying with me were your drive, your maturity, and your business sense. Do you know how many dancers have those qualities?"

I was floored. And flattered. I couldn't remember the last time someone had complimented me on something other than my looks.

"Here's what I'm proposing," Ms. Gregory said. "I need you to take on some of my classes and help me run the business. I wanted to position my studio as a finishing school for girls heading to Broadway—or Vegas, I guess. I have some connections with the junior Broadway folks, and they are looking for a feeder program. That could be us. And maybe you could tap your Vegas connections?"

"This is really exciting, Ms. Gregory," I said. "But I don't have any money to invest."

"Call me Diane," she said. "We're partners, now, right? I don't need any additional investment. The school is already open and cash flow positive. I just need help growing the business. I've been trying to do everything myself and there's some things I'm just not good at."

"When do you need me to start?" I asked. "I need to give notice at Elaine's."

"Of course," Diane said. "I'm taking reservations for the summer program, which starts June fifteenth. Would June first work? Then we could nail down the summer program and start developing the marketing strategy."

Eighteen

DANCE PROGRAM, MARKETING STRATEGY—MY HEAD WAS spinning. I felt like I was waking up from a bad dream and suddenly felt hopeful for the first time since I'd kissed Orchid goodbye.

"I'm in," I said. "This all sounds wonderful but I'm not so sure about feeding girls to the sharks in Vegas," I said.

"What, you think there are no sharks on Broadway?" Diane asked.

We laughed and lifted our coffee cups in salute.

"Here's to feeding the sharks," Diane said.

///

I gave Guido notice and started packing.

"I'll miss you," Claudia said as she hugged me. "But I'm really happy for you."

"I'm not going to be so far away," I said. "I'll come down and hang with you on weekends."

"I'm opening my studio in Philly in the fall, but I'd like to hang onto the cottage," she said.

"Count me in," I said. "I'll split the rent with you. It will be a great getaway. I'll be back living with Mom for a while."

"That's rough," Claudia said. "Living with Mom, am I right?"

"Did you ever tell your mom about your abortion?" I asked.

"No," she said. "I was so ashamed."

"I'm so sorry," I said. I held her tight. "I'm glad I could be here for you. I don't think I've ever been this close to anyone before."

//

That first Monday that I showed up for work, I felt that all of my dreams had come true. Diane had already etched my name on the door: *Jasmine Walker, Associate Director*. For the second time in my life, I felt blessed and ever so grateful. Someone had looked at me, recognized my potential, and offered me an awesome opportunity. This time I wasn't going to take any chances. I blamed myself for my mistakes—succumbing to temptation—the invitation to Eddie's party, the sexy outfit he paid for from Rousso's. I would never wear that dress again. Like the dress of a bride jilted at the altar, it hung accusingly in my closet, still soiled and stained with sweat. It was my Scarlet Letter and a constant reminder of Orchid, more poignant than her framed photo on my nightstand.

I upgraded my wardrobe—for inside the dance studio as well as outside of the office. I wanted to be seen as a polished businesswoman and never again be viewed as someone to take advantage of.

I enrolled at the College of New Jersey to finish my accounting degree and registered for some marketing courses as well.

Diane proved to be a visionary and we discovered that I was good at execution. Dance schools in the greater New York City area were a dime a dozen as were the aspiring stars. But Diane had discovered a way to bring together the demand and supply for young dancers. She called our school "Broadway Connect" and all of our classes quickly sold out. That allowed us to become more selective and we started requiring auditions, only accepting the most promising students. The strategy paid off. We began to build a reputation in New York and as far away as Los Angeles as an elite school and a reliable source of talent.

I loved being around the girls, the pre-teens especially. They were still babies and had yet to develop the cattiness and sassy backtalk of the older girls. The younger ones looked up to me and seemed to bask in individual attention. I wondered about their home lives and what made them act so needy.

My favorite was Greta. She was ten, with strawberry hair and freckles. She still carried a little baby fat, but she was showing real talent and she was a hard worker. She would hang around the studio after class and help me tidy up. She liked to run the Swiffer around the dance floor.

"What's up with your ride?" I asked. "Why are you always here late?"

"My dad is coming from work," she said. "He texted me—he's on his way."

"What about your mom?" I asked.

"She died," Greta said. "When I was seven."

"Oh, I'm so sorry," I said. "Do you have brothers and sisters?"

"No, just me," she said.

"What does your dad do?" I asked.

"He's an engineer," Greta replied. "He works for the city."

Just then, the buzzer went off and I walked out

to open the front door. Greta's dad stood there. He had her red, wavy hair and freckles. He was tall and lean; he looked like an athlete.

"You must be Greta's dad? She's just gathering her things," I said. "I'm Jasmine." I extended my hand and he took it. His palms were soft.

"Tadge," he said.

"I'm sorry?"

"That's my name—Tadge," he said. "It's Dutch."

"Wow," I said. "Cool name."

"Jasmine is pretty cool, too," he said.

I realized that he was still holding my hand and my face started to get hot.

Greta came running out and he dropped my hand.

"Well, here she is," I said, feeling stupid.

Greta pushed past us and headed toward the car. "C'mon Dad, let's go," she said. "Bye, Ms. Walker! See you next week."

"Bye, Greta. Bye, Tadge," I said.

As I locked up the office, I couldn't stop thinking about Tadge and those freckles, even though he must have been twice my age.

///

As I got ready for bed that night, I thought about Greta growing up without a mother. And that made me wonder about Orchid and what kind of girl she would grow up to be. I decided I needed to see her again.

I logged onto Facebook. There she was. With each passing day, Orchid looked more like me, except for those crazy blue eyes. That was pure Eddie. *Hey, baby*, I thought. *I'm coming back. Mommy is coming back.*

I sent Allison a private message: "Thanks for the invite to Orchid's first birthday party. I'd like to come."

Allison didn't respond right away. I imagined her discussing her reservations with Griffin. He didn't seem to be on Facebook. Maybe Allison hadn't told him that we were friends. Maybe Allison had forgotten that we were Facebook friends. Maybe she meant to post the photos not for me, but for her own extended family. I imagined the argument they were having right now. Maybe they were regretting agreeing to the open adoption.

The family! Oh, my God, I hadn't thought about Allison's family. Maybe they would all be at the party. Undoubtedly, they didn't want to meet the birth mother. Suddenly I realized how awkward this could be for Allison. Who knows what she had told her family about me? What should be a joyous celebration—Orchid's first birthday—suddenly could devolve into a drama worthy of reality TV. I started to think that the concept of open adoption was really a scam to lure scared and vulnerable young women into giving up their babies. The adopting family would prefer to slam the door and raise their child in blissful ignorance.

I thought back to Caroline's first words when I had walked into the agency.

"How old?" Caroline had asked.

"Two months," I said.

"Perfect," Caroline had said.

It was perfect because Orchid would have no memory of me, no memory of any mother other than Allison.

I slammed my laptop shut in anger.

I texted Claudia on my phone: What was I thinking? I'll never see Orchid again!

Claudia: What happened?

Me: I sent Allison a message telling her I wanted to be at Orchid's birthday party

Claudia: And?

Me: No response

Claudia: Maybe she's not online right now. Chill

Me: Maybe ur right. K

Claudia: Meet you in Cape May this weekend?

Me: Sure. I'll drive down on Saturday

Nineteen

CLAUDIA HAD OPENED HER PILATES STUDIO IN PHILADELPHIA and her business was growing.

"Look at us, the successful business owners," Claudia said. We were lounging on beach chairs and sharing a chilled bottle of Portuguese wine.

"This is the life," I said.

Except what I was really feeling was a gaping emptiness. All the visible trappings of success— your name on the door, a waiting of list of eager clients, respect in the dance community—none of it could fill the hole in my heart, the loss of my baby. Nothing seemed important to me—market share, savings in the bank—none of it really made life worth living. What felt meaningful was getting up every morning to Orchid's smile and knowing that she needed me. I desperately needed her too. What had I done?

"I'm so proud of you," I said. "Your studio—is it everything you'd hoped it would be?"

Claudia's next words came as a shock.

"I think I'd be happier being a mom," she said.

I burst into tears. "Me too!"

Claudia jumped up to hold me and rock me in her arms.

When we had both calmed down, I asked the big question: "Are you seeing anybody?"

"All of my clients are middle-aged women," Claudia said. "The UPS guy is looking pretty hot, though."

We burst into laughter.

"There's this guy—the father of my student, Greta," I said. "His wife died a few years ago. I think he's kind of hot."

"How old is he?" Claudia asked.

"I don't know—maybe thirty-six?" I guessed.

"Too old!" Claudia said.

"No," I protested. "He's in great shape—no gray hair. He must be some kind of athlete. I can't remember the last time I flirted with someone."

"It'll come back to you," she said.

//

That evening, back at the cottage, I logged onto Facebook and there it was—a message from Allison.

"We're planning a picnic in the park on Sunday the twentieth," Allison wrote. "Just family and a couple of playmates from Gymboree. We'd love it if you could join us."

"Claudia!" I screamed. "She wrote back!"

We jumped up and down in joy. Claudia cranked up her iPod and we danced to Earth, Wind & Fire.

I woke up before the alarm went off on Monday. Greta came to class on Monday and I was excited at the possibility of seeing Tadge again. With that in mind, I selected a particularly flattering violet-colored leotard with a plunging neckline. Oh, yeah, he will notice me, I thought.

Monday was our busiest day. In between classes, I got caught up in the details of billing and receivables and scheduling. Tadge had completely slipped my mind until Greta showed up at five.

I wondered how I was going to connect with him, but I needn't have worried. He arrived before class was over and stood in the corner of the studio watching. Watching Greta? Watching me? Who knew? But I was definitely watching him.

He lingered as the other children packed up and raced out to meet their parents.

"Greta's getting changed," I said. "She'll be out in a minute."

"You're really great with the girls," Tadge said. "Greta adores you."

"Tweens," I said. "That's my favorite age—so worldly and yet so innocent at the same time. I'm sorry about her mom—your wife, I mean."

"Thanks," he said. "The other driver was drunk—he walked away. Thank God, Greta made it out."

"Greta was in the car?" I asked.

"She was asleep in the back seat," he said. "That's probably what saved her. She was pretty banged up but nothing broken. It was a miracle." He looked off over my shoulder and was quiet for a minute. Then he said, "Hey, I don't mean to keep you—you must have stuff to do?"

Nothing more important than talking to you, I thought to myself.

Just then, Greta came bounding out and lunged at her dad.

"Bye, you guys," I said.

On Wednesday, Tadge showed up again, a few minutes before six. Again, he stood in the corner near the door and watched the class.

I dismissed the girls and walked over to him.

"Tadge, I have a question," I said. This brilliant idea had come to me during the last five minutes of class. "We are putting together a fund-raiser and I was hoping that Greta could perform. It would mean extra rehearsals on Friday evenings and Saturday afternoons for a few weeks. Is that alright with you?"

"Is there a cost?" he asked.

"No," I said. "But, we will need help selling tickets. Maybe you can sell some tickets at your office?"

"I work for the city," he said. "So that's a little complicated. But I can hit up my running club."

"You're a runner?" I asked. *That explains your physique*, I thought.

"I was a gymnast in college, actually," Tadge said. "These days I stick to running." He pulled out his phone and opened his calendar. "When will rehearsals start? This Friday?"

"Not this week," I said. "I need to talk to the other parents. I'll email you. Do I have your email?" Tadge followed me into the office. I dug my phone out of my purse and typed in his name. He spelled out his email address.

"So you're a non-profit?" he asked.

"The fund-raiser isn't for us—we're doing it for the Children's Hospital," I said. "But it's great experience for the girls and the school gets some publicity out of it."

"Very nice," he said. "Hey, would you like to grab coffee sometime?" he asked. "I mean if you're not seeing anyone." He blushed. "I'm sorry. I don't have a lot of experience at this."

"No . . . yes," I said. "No, I'm not seeing anyone, and yes, I'd love to grab coffee." Claudia was right. This was easier than I had expected.

"Great!" he said. "Saturday morning? Do you have a favorite spot?"

"Warehouse Café is nice," I said.

"Meet you there at nine-thirty?" Tadge asked.

"Sure," I said.

I tried hard but I couldn't remember the last time I had been out on a date. There was that guy Joey, freshman year, but he just wanted to hook up and I wasn't that into him. This was like grown-up dating.

Twenty

"**I** FEEL LIKE I CAN TALK TO YOU." TADGE HAD FOUND A table on the sidewalk outside the café. "People act so weird around me," he continued. "Yes, my wife died in a tragic accident. But life has to go on—for Greta, for me, right? Am I right?"

"I think people mean well," I said. "They just don't know what to say."

"You seem different, though," Tadge said. "Have you experienced loss?"

Wow! Is this the kind of topic you bring up on a first date? Where was Claudia when I needed her? Advice, please!

"You're not a small-talk kind of guy, I take it?"

I asked, hoping I didn't sound flippant. To my relief, he laughed. I really liked his laugh.

"This is what I mean," he said. "You make me laugh. Greta makes me laugh. But there aren't enough people out there who know how to laugh. You are really special. Greta thinks the world of you."

"The admiration is mutual," I said. "Greta reminds me of myself at that age. She's got talent, and more importantly, she has drive."

"Were you on Broadway?" Tadge asked. "No, wait, your bio on the website says something about Las Vegas."

"You checked out my bio?" I asked.

Tadge blushed and his entire neck and face turned beet-red. Oh my God, this guy was adorable!

"Well, of course you wanted to check out the background of your daughter's dance teacher," I said. "That just makes sense. Yes, I was a Vegas showgirl."

"Was?" he asked. "You're retired? You're so young."

"A young dancer's dream is to perform," I said. "But, I've found my true calling. Sure, it was exciting, and if they called me tomorrow and offered me a starring role, I probably wouldn't turn it down. But I find teaching so much more rewarding. It may be hard to understand, but I get a lot more respect as a teacher than I ever did as a dancer."

"I totally understand that," Tadge said.

I was feeling really safe with Tadge, so I said, "I didn't mean to dodge the question. I have experienced loss. I'm going through a terrible loss as we speak. I lost my child. I can't seem to get over it."

I shared the story of Orchid, not everything of course. The whole Eddie story could wait for later.

"I don't like to talk about this," I said. "I always end up crying. I'm sorry."

"Don't be sorry," he said. "You need to talk about it. And I'm glad you picked me."

"Do you think I did the right thing?" I asked.

"The Martins sound wonderful," he said. "I'm not sure there is one 'right' thing, but you definitely made a good decision."

"Thank you for understanding," I said.

"Of course," he said. "When will you see her again?"

"Her birthday is in September," I said. "Allison invited me to come."

"Are you excited?"

"Terrified," I said.

///

On Monday, I approached Diane.

"What's up, Jasmine?" she said.

"I'd like to take a few days off in September," I said.

"Geez, J," she said. "That's our busy month, with classes starting up and all."

"I know," I said. "Just three days, the nineteenth

through the twenty-second. I'll be back in time for classes on Tuesday. It's really important. I have some unfinished business in Las Vegas."

"Las Vegas?" Diane said. "Actually, this would be a good opportunity to build some awareness for our school. Why don't you do some networking while you're out there?"

//

I arrived in Las Vegas on Saturday afternoon and was met at McCarran Airport by the driver for Hotel32, the boutique hotel on top of the Monte Carlo. Staring out the car window at my old haunts, nothing looked like it had changed, but I didn't recognize myself. One year before, I was a broke, pregnant teen working at a car wash. I was returning in style, traveling on an expense account.

Diane expected me to network, but I really didn't know anybody in the business other than

Eddie, Geri, Ginger, Katrina—maybe Kent, the assistant director; I think I still had his email.

As soon as I checked in, I went online and bought a ticket to the late show of *Bacchanal*. Then I sent emails to Eddie, Kent and Geri.

> Hi, I'm in town for a few days and I'd love to catch up over a drink. I'm running a dance school in the New York City area. We're developing young talent for Broadway and I wanted to discuss opportunities to develop a pipeline for shows on the Strip. Let me know if you have some time to meet later this afternoon or tomorrow after five.
> Cheers,
> Jazz

Wow! That was not the voice of the scared little coed who had bared her breasts for a shot at a gig in a hit show.

I guess I shouldn't have been surprised when

every single one of them responded—"Great to hear from you. Let's get together. Where are you staying?"—that sort of thing. But I attributed my success to Diane's genius. "Pipeline"—everyone needs a pipeline. I imagined opening branches of Broadway Connect in L.A. and Chicago.

I made appointments with Kent and Geri to meet at the pool bar between five and eight. I told Eddie I would meet him after the late show at Bally's. Then I booked a massage and a mani-pedi.

//

I slipped into a sleek Kenneth Cole outfit—pencil slacks and flowing sleeveless blouse and the strappy sandals from that fateful night. I knew I looked like a million bucks as I strode confidently toward the pool bar. The *maître-d'* escorted me to a pool-side table. I ordered glass of Prosecco and toasted to my good luck.

I saw Kent approach and waved him over. I stood to greet him.

"Hi, I'm Jasmine," I said, extending my hand. "We met once about a year ago?"

"Yes, of course," Kent said. "I remember. In Eddie's office."

"How are things going?" I asked.

"I'm no longer working with Eddie," Kent said. "It's a bit of a revolving-door there. I was intrigued by your email. I'm sure you're aware of our demographic problem—too many blue hairs in the audience, if you know what I mean. We're putting together a show to attract more millennials to the Strip. We're going for the *Glee* audience. I've been tasked with finding young talent. Your feeder program sounds perfect. Maybe we could collaborate on the curriculum?"

I was no longer hearing Kent's words. I was floating on air and dreaming about the possibility of monthly visits to Las Vegas for "business" that would allow me to see Orchid regularly.

Just then, Geri approached the table.

I rose. "Geri, do you know Kent?" I asked.

They greeted each other and air-kissed.

Before he left, Kent and I exchanged cards and scheduled a call for the following week.

Geri sat down.

"How are you?" Geri asked. "You look amazing. I'm so sorry that we lost touch after you left the show. You're obviously feeling better."

"I was pregnant, Geri," I said. I immediately regretted saying that. I didn't want to give her any details—about Eddie, or giving Orchid up for adoption. I didn't want to say that I was in town for her birthday party. The high I had been feeling a minute before was gone. I suddenly felt like shit.

Twenty one

"**W**ELL, IT LOOKS LIKE YOU'VE REBOUNDED," GERI SAID. "I wish I could say the same for myself."

"What are you up to?" I asked.

"Since Eddie fired me, I've been freelancing, looking for work," Geri said. "When I got your email, I thought maybe there is some way we could work together. I know every producer and director in town. Your idea of building a feeder school is absolutely brilliant."

"I wish I could take credit," I said. "My partner, Diane, came up with it. But it is a good idea, isn't it? Funny, Kent said the same thing—the old way of finding talent by posting fliers around town or announcing casting calls on Backstage.com is so random, right? What if we could cultivate talent via a network of training schools and talent scouts?"

We agreed to set up a call with Diane the following week to nail down the financial arrangements of a partnership.

Geri gave me a big hug. "It's great to see that you're doing so well," she said.

I paid the bill with my corporate card and went back upstairs to my room to rest before the ten o'clock show.

I texted Diane: Great meetings here. I'll schedule follow-up calls for Tuesday when I'm back

I lay down on the bed, and the next thing I knew my alarm was going off. Shit, nine p.m. already? I needed to fix my face and get dressed. I had brought a silver sequined sheath—not something I'd ever wear in New Jersey, but it was perfect for Vegas. I touched up my hair and makeup and rushed downstairs where my driver was waiting to take me to Bally's. The line at will-call was long and I just barely made it to my table before the house lights dimmed.

Bacchanal! I had never been in the audience before. The music swelled and the showgirls strutted out. Wow! It really was exciting. When it came to my part in the show where the set opened to reveal the dark-skinned, half-clothed beauties, shimmying and high-kicking to reveal a glimpse of what might have been their naked pussies, the crowd gasped, gratified that their money had been well-spent. *Geez, Eddie*, I thought, *this is really hot!*

//

Eddie had agreed to meet at the Indigo Lounge at eleven-thirty. I got there early and found a table near the window with a spectacular view of the Strip. I ordered a diet ginger ale and nervously fingered the straw in my glass while I waited for him.

I saw him the moment he entered the bar; his graceful swagger was unmistakable. I watched him as he crossed the room, looking expectantly around him. He sized up the girls to his left and right as he advanced toward my table.

Suddenly I realized what a bad idea this was. *What does he want?* I wondered. For that matter, what did I want?

"Eddie, hi." I rose to greet him.

"Jazz," he said. "You're looking amazing as ever." He waved the waiter over and ordered a dry martini.

"So, what are you up to?" he asked. He looked me straight in the eye and I couldn't even imagine what he was thinking.

"As I said in my message, I'm running a dance school in New York." I said. "My partner, Diane, and I thought there might be a need for a feeder program for young talent." I couldn't get the visual out of my head—feeding young, impressionable young girls to a shark that had Eddie's face.

"I don't actually know that many people on the

Strip," I said. "So I thought I'd reach out to you and see if you could make some intros for me."

"Happy to," he said. "I know Kent Robbins is working on a show targeting a younger audience— this could be good fit."

"Yes," I said. "I met with Kent."

"You did?" He sounded surprised. "How do you know Kent?"

Had he no memory of our last meeting?

"Well," he continued. "I don't take girls younger than eighteen, so that won't work."

Take girls, I thought. *That's an interesting choice of words. Like you took me?*

"Let me think about it," he said as he finished his drink. "If I hear of something, I'll call you."

I was dying to bring up Orchid and tell him that his daughter was a year old. But then I thought better of it. He might track her down. God knows he had the resources. He would find the Martins and make their life a living hell.

"Thanks, Eddie," I said. "I would appreciate it."

I watched him walk out of the bar, and suddenly I pitied him. Sure, he had money and fame. But he had no love in his heart.

//

On Sunday morning, I woke up confused, unsure of where I was, and wondering what this weird feeling in my chest was. Then I remembered. I was going to see Orchid today. How was I going to control my emotions? I didn't want to get all weepy in front of everyone. And how was I going to restrain my urge to snatch her and make a run for it?

As I showered and dressed, I worried about the outfit I had chosen. I had packed Kate Spade Capri pants and a cropped tee, wanting to look like a responsible adult, not some slutty teen mom. But what did that say to Orchid? If I was so successful, why did I abandon my baby? Part of me thought I should tart it up—cut-off jeans, a halter-top— playing the part of the loser mom.

"She won't remember this," I said out loud. And that thought brought tears to my eyes. What if I hadn't panicked and called Dr. Bergen? What if I had just packed up and drove to New Jersey with Orchid tucked into her car seat? How could I have known that within a year I would be co-owner of a successful dance studio, clearing enough cash to pay for rent and day care?

Hold it together, girl, I ordered myself. I packed my purse, double-checking to see if I had my room key, rental car keys, iPhone, and plenty of Kleenex.

I pulled into the parking lot of the county park, not sure where I would find the party. I checked my make-up in the mirror. "Are you really doing this?" I asked my reflection.

I locked the car and started strolling across the park. I decided the Kate Spade outfit made me appear less threatening, just part of the suburban scenery.

And then I saw them—a happy, boisterous gathering. The older kids were running around, attempting to launch a bright blue-and-yellow kite. I stood and observed them from a distance. The adults were seated on a checkered blanket, drinking from red Solo cups. There she was. Orchid sat in Allison's lap, happily banging a Solo cup on the ground, bang, bang, bang.

She spoke first. "Jasmine, hi!" Allison shouted across the lawn.

I sucked in my breath and strode bravely toward them, holding my emotions in check.

"You look great," Allison said.

"Thanks," I said. "Orchid looks wonderful."

"Sit," Allison said. "Let me make you a plate. Can you hold her?"

Can I hold her? I thought. *Can I hold my baby? Shit, yeah, I can hold her!*

Allison handed Orchid to me as she busily filled a plate with fried chicken, potato salad, baked beans and coleslaw.

"Hi, baby," I said to Orchid. I attempted to snuggle her, but she struggled in my arms and reached for Allison. She'll recognize me in a minute, I thought—my smell, my touch. I tried to kiss her but she turned her face away. I felt such distress as I realized that Orchid was no longer mine; she had bonded with Allison.

I handed Orchid back to Allison and took the plate of food. I made a show of pushing the food around with my plastic fork as Allison introduced her sister, her neighbor and the kids, but my stomach was in a knot. I had no appetite. I couldn't keep my eyes off of Orchid, and I felt Griffin's eyes burning a hole in the back of my head.

"Let me get a group shot," he said, aiming his iPhone at me and Allison with Orchid perched between us.

"This will be a nice memory for her," Allison said. "Baby's first birthday with both of her mommies."

It dawned on me how generous Allison was— inviting me to share this moment. She was a good person, and Orchid was very lucky to have her.

I didn't stay long. I made some excuse about meeting some friends. Allison walked me to my car with Orchid in her arms.

"Someday I want to have a family," I said. I stroked Orchid's head and she buried her face in Allison's chest. "And I hope to be as good a mom as you." I started to cry. "Hell, I'd like to be as good a person as you."

"Group hug," Allison said, embracing me with her free arm.

On my way back to the hotel I texted Tadge and he called an hour later.

"How did it go?" he asked.

I fought back tears. "I've lost her," I said.

"Come home," he said.

Twenty two

TADGE PICKED ME UP AT NEWARK AIRPORT AND WE drove to his house. He lived in Guttenberg in a house overlooking the Hudson with an amazing view of Manhattan from his living room. The vehicles on the West Side Highway looked like Matchbox cars whizzing by.

"What a view!" I said.

"My great-grandfather built this house in the twenties." he said.

"Where's Greta?" I asked.

"She's at a sleepover," Tadge said. "We're all alone tonight. Would you like a glass of wine? And maybe a tour of the house?"

I followed Tadge upstairs to peek into Greta's room. I asked to use the bathroom and he led me through the master bedroom to the master bath. Inside, there was an enormous claw-foot tub.

"Tadge," I said. I found him downstairs in the living room. "This is going to sound crazy, but would you mind if I took a bath? It's been a really stressful day."

"Sure," he said. "Let me get you some towels and the bubble bath that Greta got for Christmas."

Tadge carried my bag upstairs and laid the towels and a clean robe on the bed.

"You know that's a two-person tub," he said.

"Would you like to join me?" I asked.

Tadge drew the bath and we climbed into the steamy bubbles together. I sat between his legs and rested my back against his chest. He gently massaged my neck and shoulders.

"This is heaven," I said.

"I know," he said.

"I need to get her back," I said.

"Orchid?" he asked. "Let's go over the adoption papers tomorrow and see what the possibilities are. She's been with the Martins for nine months already. It may be too late."

"I thought about that," I said. "But the father never gave consent."

"You know who the father is?" Tadge asked.

"I'm pretty sure," I said.

"Does he know about Orchid?" he asked.

"Yeah, he knows," I said. "And he threatened me that he'd file for full custody if I filed a paternity suit. I was scared—I had no money to fight him in court. When I realized I couldn't take care of her, adoption seemed like the only option. But, I'm doing so much better now."

"Who is this asshole?" Tadge asked.

"His name is Eddie Watson," I said. "He was the director of the show." I shared the whole story of the dress, the party, the pool, the pills and waking up in Eddie's bed.

"Let's go out there next weekend and see him,"

Tadge said. "If he threatens you again, we'll threaten him with a rape charge."

"You'll come with me?" I asked.

"Of course," he said. "We're in this together."

He wrapped me in his arms and held me until the water started to cool.

"Let me get you a towel," he said as he climbed out of the tub. "Do you want to stay over?"

"Yes," I said.

//

That night I had sex for the first time since, oh my God, I couldn't even remember. Since, of course, I didn't remember actually having sex with Eddie. I didn't even realize how much I had missed it—I hadn't really thought about dating since Orchid was born. Tadge fell asleep with his arms wrapped around me so tight I had a hard time sleeping. But it was so soothing to lie in his embrace and listen to his soft breathing. *I think I love this man!*

In the morning, over coffee and toast, Tadge booked us two tickets to Las Vegas.

"What's the best way to do this?" he asked.

"The show is dark on Friday and Sunday," I said. "Last week I was able to meet him after the Saturday show, but I don't think we want to do this in a bar. I'll see if I can schedule a meeting in his office on Saturday or Sunday."

"You saw him last week?" Tadge asked, surprised.

"Just about the school," I said. "Diane had asked me to do some networking while I was out there and he's one of only a handful of people I know in the business. Not that he was helpful, he doesn't work with girls younger than eighteen."

"And he didn't ask about the baby?" Tadge asked.

"No," I said. "Every time I've seen him, he

always acted like he had no memory of the last time. He's a weird dude."

"Do you think he'll help us?" Tadge asked.

"He's my only shot at getting her back," I said.

I texted Eddie: I need a favor. Can we meet on Saturday at your office?

An hour later, Eddie replied. Come to the house Saturday afternoon. Around 3?

I replied: Thanks. See you then

///

We flew out of Newark on Saturday morning.

"I spoke with a family law attorney in Las Vegas," Tadge said.

"You did?" I asked. I was very impressed with his planning and organization skills. Must be the engineer in him!

"We're meeting with this guy, Neil Mullins, this afternoon at one." Tadge said. "I explained your situation. If you can get Eddie to agree to contest the adoption, Mullins can take care of everything. Let Mullins prep you before you talk to Eddie."

//

We landed just before noon and took a cab straight to the attorney's office.

Once we were settled into the conference room and had exchanged pleasantries, Mr. Mullins asked me to go over the story again.

"So to sum it up, Ms. Walker," Mr. Mullins said. "Mr. Watson knows what happened on the evening of December eighteenth. He also knows that you gave birth on September twenty-first."

"That is correct," I said. "There is a possibility that he is not the father, but I really doubt it. Katrina—she was one of the dancers in the show—she pretty much confirmed for me that Eddie was alone with me that night."

"And," Mr. Mullins continued. "Mr. Watson threatened you with a custody suit if you filed a paternity suit. How do we know he doesn't want custody?"

"If he wanted custody, he would have already filed a suit," Tadge said. "He just wants to avoid financial responsibility."

"Correct," Mr. Mullins said. "And you're willing to waive his parental responsibilities in exchange for his help in contesting the adoption?"

"Yes," I said. "I don't need anything from him."

"But Mr. Watson was never informed of the adoption, correct?" Mr. Mullins said.

"Correct," I said. "Technically I had no proof of paternity, so no paternal consent was required."

"Are the Martins aware of any of this?" Mr. Mullins asked.

"Yes," I said.

"Yes?" Tadge exclaimed. "You never told me that part!"

"I told Allison," I said. "I didn't want Orchid to grow up thinking I was some slut who didn't know who her father was."

"That's great," Mr. Mullins said. "That will make everything easier. So here is our approach. You're meeting Mr. Watson at three this afternoon?"

I nodded.

Twenty three

MR. MULLINS CONTINUED. "YOU NEED TO CONVINCE Mr. Watson that A) you are releasing him from all financial responsibility, B) you were desperate and signed the adoption papers under duress. You regret the decision, and the only way you can get your daughter back is with his help. He will never hear from you or your daughter again without his explicit consent."

Tadge was taking notes.

"Do not get emotional," Mr. Mullins said. "Do not make any accusations of raping or drugging you or anything else. Convince him that whether or not he is the father, you need his help to get your daughter back. Once we prove paternity and his attorney files a claim with the court, it will be a slam-dunk."

"Tell him we will cover all of his legal fees, too," Tadge said.

"Have his attorney call me," Mr. Mullins said as he handed me his card. "We can file all the paperwork this week and have your child back in your arms soon."

"Oh my God," I cried.

"Honey, don't get emotional," Tadge reminded me. "You need to be cool with this dude. Don't give him any reason to feel threatened."

"What if he refuses?" I asked.

"We can force the paternity test and legally overturn the adoption on the basis of fraud," Mr. Mullins said. "It might get a little ugly. You'd be accused of fraudulently submitting a petition for adoption. The judge will be forced to rule in your favor, but it could get a little unpleasant. You'd have to face the Martins in court and admit that you suspected that Eddie was the father but didn't seek his consent. You would be forced to plead poverty and ignorance, and that will all be in the public record for Orchid to discover one day. However, since you told Allison the whole story, that makes the Martins party to the fraud."

"If Eddie agrees to help, I won't have to face Allison?" I asked.

"No, the lawyers will handle all the proceedings and the court will appoint a social worker to pick up Orchid and bring her to you."

//

The cab pulled up in front of Eddie's house.

"Wow," Tadge said. "This place is a mansion. Are you sure you don't want to sue him for child support too?"

"No!" I punched Tadge in the arm.

"I'm just kidding," he said, rubbing his arm.

"I'll be waiting at the hotel. Text me and I'll have a cab pick you up."

"I love you," I said. "I couldn't have done this without you."

"We haven't done anything yet," he said. "Good luck, sweetie." He gave me a long, deep kiss.

I walked up the steps to the front porch and rang the doorbell. I held my breath until I heard footsteps.

A man I didn't recognize answered the door.

"Hello," I said. "I have an appointment with Eddie."

"Harold Lessing," he said. "I'm Eddie's attorney. Follow me, please."

"I'm glad you're here," I said. I followed Mr. Lessing down the hallway to Eddie's study. Eddie was sitting on a leather sofa with his legs crossed, smoking a thin cigar.

"Hi Eddie," I said. "Thanks so much for meeting me."

"Jazz," he said. "Have a seat. How can I help you?"

Once we were all seated, I cleared my throat and started in. "I need a favor, Eddie. I made a terrible mistake. After I saw you in December at your office, when I brought Orchid, do you remember? You told me that I would lose custody because I had no money? Well, you were right. I gave Orchid up for adoption because I couldn't take care of her on my own, and I didn't know what else to do."

"And what do you want from me, now?" Eddie asked.

"Eddie, I assume you know who the father is?" I said. "I need the father to file a petition for paternity with the court to overturn the adoption. I don't care who the father is—I don't want any financial support—I'll sign any waiver that he requires." I looked at Mr. Lessing as I said this. "When I signed the adoption papers, I stipulated that I didn't know who the father was—and I don't. But the father knows who he is and he deserved the right to consent to the adoption. Only the father can overturn the adoption. I want my baby back, that's all I'm asking for. We'll pay all of your attorney fees."

"Do you have an attorney?" Mr. Lessing asked.

"Yes." I dug Mr. Mullins' card out of my purse.

He read the card. "Neil Mullins. I know him. I've met him at Bar Association meetings," he said to Eddie. "We can settle this quickly and quietly."

To me he asked, "You're willing to release my client from all financial responsibility?"

"Yes," I said.

"And he will never hear from you or your daughter again without his explicit consent?" he asked.

"Those were Mr. Mullins' exact words!" I exclaimed. "Yes, absolutely."

//

I sat on a wrought iron bench on Eddie's front porch and waited for the taxi. When the driver pulled up, I saw Tadge in the back seat.

"How did I it go?" Tadge asked as I slid in beside him.

"He agreed to do it!" I said. "His attorney was there, and he took Mr. Mullins' card and said they would settle everything quickly."

"So that creep admitted that he raped you?" Tadge asked.

"No," I said. "Nobody admitted anything. The attorney kept referring to his client. I don't care about that; I don't care about Eddie. I just want Orchid back."

Just then, Tadge's phone rang.

"Tell Jasmine she did a great job," Mr. Mullins said. "Harold Lessing just called. Mr. Watson is cooperating. We'll petition the Martins for a DNA sample on Monday and file the paternity suit. I'll draft up the waiver agreement. You need to prepare Jasmine—the Martins are going to be very upset when they receive the summons. They may lash out at her. Tell her to refrain from engaging with Mrs. Martin on Facebook. We need to keep all communications at arm's length. Let the attorneys handle it."

Tadge hung up. "You did it," he said. "You're getting Orchid back." I leapt into his arms.

"When?" I asked.

"I don't know, sweetie," he said. "It could take a few weeks, I suppose. I can't wait to meet her. Greta is excited too. Will you move in with us?"

Twenty four

NEVER HEARD FROM ALLISON AGAIN. SHE HAD QUIETLY unfriended me on Facebook, but before she did I saw that she had removed all traces of Orchid. I felt very sad for her. I hope she knew that I got no joy from her loss. I felt only love for her. It was obvious that she loved Orchid and she was the best possible adoptive mother a girl could hope for.

I think about the Martins all the time. They probably think about Orchid, too.

Her attorney told Mr. Mullins that Allison wasn't surprised to hear from Eddie Watson. She said she'd always known it was a possibility that he would track Orchid down and claim paternity. She surrendered custody without putting up a fight, but I knew that her heart was broken. I wondered what Griffin thought about everything. I don't think he ever trusted me and I hope he had steeled himself for the worst.

Tadge and I had to fly to Vegas one last time, several weeks later, to sign all of the paperwork. As promised, a social worker delivered Orchid to Mr. Mullins' office. She was so big! She no longer recognized me and was fussy all the way home on the plane, which broke my heart and disturbed many of our fellow passengers. But I kept reminding myself that it was only natural. It would take time to renew our bond. I was hoping to breastfeed her, but my milk had dried up long before. She had to settle for warmed-up bottles of formula and lots of walking up and down the aisle of the plane. Eventually, she fell asleep, exhausted from all the crying.

Sometimes life just happens to you and it feels like you are wandering through a maze with no end goal in site. And then you look back and try to make sense of it all—it appears that you can draw a straight line from point A to point B.

I had wanted to be a dancer from the minute I could stand up. Mom had home videos of me boogieing in my playpen to music on the stereo. I begged her to enroll me in ballet classes when I was five and then tap when I was eight and jazz when I was ten. I was star-struck the first time I saw a Broadway show, and I was determined to make it. And I *had* made it—all the way to Bally's—picked out of the crowd by none other than the world-famous Eddie Watson.

I did not plan on having a baby, obviously! Who does, when you're a teenager in college? But I believe I was a good mother, a very good mother, until the day I realized I couldn't be the mother that my baby needed. So I found a better mother for her. But then, through the love and support of Claudia, Diane and Tadge, I found the strength to fight to get my daughter back.

I wondered what I would tell Orchid about her first year, if anything. That's what troubles me most. When Orchid asks about her father, and of course she will ask about her father, what will I tell her? Let's just take for granted that she will be an amazingly talented dancer, or maybe even a choreographer. Sure, I could take all of the genetic credit and tell her that I didn't know who her dad was or that her dad drove a bus for New Jersey Transit. Or I could show her photos of Eddie. She would know in an instant that she had his eyes. But, legally we had agreed not to contact him. There were probably other Orchids out there—other babies that Eddie had fathered and disowned, having paid off their mothers in one way or another. I only hoped that this wouldn't scar her for life.

There are no regrets in life. As Helen Keller said, "Life is either a daring adventure or nothing." If I had never met Eddie, I would not have my beautiful daughter, Orchid. If I had not taken